THE RIVER'S SONG

# ACKNOWLEDGMENTS

I thank the folks in the Graduate Creative Writing Program at NYU. In particular: Andre Aciman, E.L. Doctorow, Mary Gaitskill, Irini Spanidou, and, especially, Paule Marshall. For wandering on my path when I really needed them and for greeting me with enthusiasm and warmth, I thank: Catharine Stimpson, Fred Papert, and Hamilton Fish. Stacy Ann Blair, Marsha Coburn, Yvonne Knight, Dolace Nicole McLean, Veronica Mitchell, Yvonne Murphy & Sheron Witter – sisters of the yam all. Karen Singleton, thanks so much and again. Orville "Ray" Cousins, Dawn and Errol Holness; Adam and Arzu McConnel; the Marouani clan in Morocco (especially, Karim Marouani, mon amour); Alva Jacobs, Adeniyi Johnson, Clifford Mason, Ozgur Metin, Robert Rutherford, Thierno Moustapha Seydi. Merle Collins you are so very kind and so very thorough. Jeremy Poynting and Hannah Bannister you both work so hard! Thanks also to the staff and students at the Opportunity Programs at NYU, with particular thanks to Peggy Davis, for much computer assistance; Dr. Bernadette Penceal, Maureen McDonough-Kolb, and Valerie Cabral. My mother; my sisters Michelle Anne Marie and Kamara Soyini; my brothers Dave and Collin. I thank my grandmother for her humor and her warmth, my father and my step-mother; and, of course, I cannot forget the four great miracles in my life: my niece, Demaya, and my nephews, Daveon, Dimargio and Shamari – your births have all been gifts! I thank the characters for choosing me to tell their story and hope wherever in the world Nilda, Yvette, Annie and Gloria now are, comforting hands will reach for them as they have almost always reached for me. Asante Sana!

JACQUELINE BISHOP

THE RIVER'S SONG
A NOVEL

PEEPAL TREE

First published in Great Britain in 2007
Peepal Tree Press Ltd
17 King's Avenue
Leeds LS6 1QS
England

ISBN: 1 84523 038 8
ISBN13: 978 1 84523 038 8

 Peepal Tree gratefully acknowledges Arts Council support

*Sparkling, flashing, gleaming, glowing,*
*Where no eye can see its rays,*
*Rests the mystic golden table*
*Dreaming dreams of olden days.*
*'Neath the Cobre's silver water*
*It has lain for ages long;*
*And an undertone of warning*
*Mingle's with the river's song.*

~ *The Legend of the Golden Table*

*On the dresser sits a frame*
*With a photograph*
*Two little girls in ponytails*
*Some twenty one years back*

~ *Cindy Lauper, "Sally's Pigeon"*

For
Kamara & Demaya

*I went to see Annie on my last day on the island. She was sitting on a plain wooden chair in her room, looking out of the wide-open windows at the dark-blue mountains. She turned slowly and looked at me when I walked into the room, a long searching, searing look, before she looked back out the window without saying anything. Her mother, pale and ashen, kept looking from Annie to me, trying, for the umpteenth time, to figure out what had happened between us – just what had gone so terribly wrong. Getting no answer, she withdrew.*

*Annie looked down at her slender fingers. She turned to look at me again, another searing, searching look, tears rapidly filling her eyes, before she looked back out of the window. It seemed in this one moment that I was saying goodbye to so many people: to a woman named Rachel whom I had loved and who had so loved me; and to the girls, now women, who had all left their mark on me – to Junie, Sophie, Nilda, and that girl Yvette, wherever in the world she might be. I was saying goodbye to my mother, my grandmother, Zekie, the island. But most of all, I was saying goodbye to Annie. Dear sweet Annie.*

*She tried to say something, but it was too great an effort to get even a few words out. She seemed to be searching for something else to say, before she gave up, and pulled an even tighter veil over her face. She looked down, frail, emaciated, hands trembling in her lap. There was that look again on her face, of deep confusion; something just did not make any sense to her.*

*I made to go over to her, but found I could not; my feet had grown roots it seemed, down into the ground. She seemed so tiny, so frail. Annie. After that, all I could do was hurriedly leave the room, hurry down the stairs and out of the house, an anguished sob trailing behind me. This is how I remember it, years and years later. This is how I remember it, and why I had to write it down.*

7

# CHAPTER I

"I knew you could do it! I believed you would do it!" my mother said, smiling down into my face that she'd just covered with kisses.

The entire tenement yard must have heard her cry of delight as my mother danced around the tiny two rooms we lived in, thumping heavily on the dark brown wooden floor, waking up not only me, but also the insects burrowed deep into the wood. When she was done dancing she pulled me out from under the quilt my grandmother had made for me, *when-you-were-a-baby-no-bigger-than-the-palm-of-my-hand*, gathered me into her arms and started kissing me all over my face. That morning, the examination results were finally printed in the newspaper and I was one of the girls who received a scholarship to All Saints High School, the most prestigious girl's school on the island.

Outside it was cool and dark, the sounds of early morning coming into the house through the jalousie windows. Ground lizards shuffled up and down the hibiscus tree outside our door, and the crimson sun was just beginning over the horizon, rising above the dark-blue mountains, which dominated Kingston. As the sun rose, the large white mansions perched on the mountainsides came into view. These were the houses my mother often looked at with desire. One day, some way, some how, we would live in one of the houses in the hills. Then-we-would-become-somebody.

I did not know when my mother left the house to go and buy the newspaper with the examination results. I knew I had passed when I heard her screaming. All night long I twisted and turned in bed, making all sorts of deals with God if he allowed me to pass

9

my common entrance exam. I would stop telling lies and stealing money from my mother's purse to buy all manner of foolishness. I would go willingly to church every Sunday and there would be no quarrelling with my mother about how I was dragging my foot in the house instead of hurrying off to hear the word of the Lord.

"Come, come and look. Look, right here, under All Saints High School, is your name."

I rubbed my eyes, blinked, and looked where my mother was pointing her finger excitedly. Underlined twice in red-ink was my name. It was there along with the primary school I attended. A slow smile started across my face. At thirteen years old, and on my first attempt, I had gotten into All Saints. The many months of extra lesson classes, reluctantly leaving my friends on the playing field and heading off to Mrs. Porter's, had finally borne fruit.

"Come, I have something for you!" My mother took her handbag out of the closet and started rummaging inside. When she didn't find what she was looking for, she emptied the bag's contents on the table and started rifling through them. She pushed aside bills, receipts, the green lime she carried as-protection-against-things-evil, a shiny fluorescent metallic-purple make-up kit, before she finally found a small plastic bag.

"This," she said, "is for you." She tipped out the contents and there in the soft pink of her palm was a pair of gold earrings: birds in flight – red rubies for eyes, the tips of their tiny beaks a brilliant moss-green. They were the earrings I'd seen a couple weeks before in a jewellery store in downtown Kingston. I had stood for a long time just looking and looking at them. My mother had come up to the window and together we looked at the earrings, before my mother took my hand and slowly led me away. We both knew she could never afford them.

I shrieked and threw myself into my mother's arms. Laughter bubbled up from a warm soft place inside. Hugging, we danced around the room. I was happy my mother was happy. I was happy to make my mother happy. My mother wasn't always very happy with me.

"I knew you would do it!" She gave me a long satisfied look. "I just knew you would! Girl, I'm too proud of you! Now we'll have to send a letter to your grandmother to let her know the good news, though I suspect by the time the letter gets to her, she'll have heard it already – your Grandy has a way of finding out these things!"

This used to surprise me, how my grandmother would turn up just when my mother was at her wits end and needed her the most. When I was feverish and sick and my mother was distraught and crying, not knowing what to do, I would look up to see Grandy's cocoa-brown face bent low over mine. When I was younger, Grandy would visit at least once a month, but she didn't come as often any more; her arthritic feet gave her more and more problems Still, every now and again she made her way to the city to see us and I still spent all my summer holidays with her in the country.

When Grandy found out I'd passed my exam, she'd be as pleased as my mother, maybe even more so; she was forever telling me that if I wanted to become somebody-in-this-here-Jamaica-place I had to go to high school; if I did not go to high school, dog already eat my supper.

"Your grandmother will tell all of her church sisters! Everyone within a one-mile radius of her front yard will hear about you – her bright-bright granddaughter who get scholarship! Perhaps," my mother finished, on a quieter, more ominous note, "one of us *will* complete her education at All Saints High School!"

I looked closely at her, hoping she wouldn't fall into one of her moods when she blamed me and my father for not becoming the doctor she always wanted to be; not having her house in the hills. My mother had been going to All Saints, was in her last year when she met my father who twisted up her head, turned her into a fool and, before long, Mama was in-the-family-way. She was forced to leave school, and that was not the worst of it, for she had to fight with my father to acknowledge me. There was a steely determination in her face, as she repeated, "One of us *will* graduate from that school!"

There was a loud knock at the door.

"Who is it?" Mama called.

"Well, who do you expect it to be?" a woman's rough voice called back good-naturedly. "Is only me, Rachel! Let me into the house before I freeze to death out here in this cold morning air!"

Rachel was Mama's best friend in the yard and I knew, sooner or later, she would turn up at our door.

"Don't tell me," Rachel said, "Gloria pass her examination!"

Rachel was a short stout woman, very dark, wearing a pale-pink nightgown over which she'd thrown a sheet to ease off the cold. Most of the women in the yard did not like Rachel because she was a "night-woman", but Mama was friends with her, even over my grandmother's objections.

"After all," my grandmother would say in one of the heated arguments that erupted over Rachel, "You know what she does for a living! If you not careful, people might start thinking you do the same thing too!"

"When I was sick the other day, she was the only person in this yard who came to see how I was doing. Even made dinner for Gloria and me. Take her good-good money and buy us parrot-fish for dinner. I could've been dead and none of those other people came to see what was going on with me, let alone make us dinner. I telling you, Ma' Louise," Mama raised her voice so the other people in the yard could hear, "Rachel is the only genuine person in this place!"

"Just a little flu, nothing much!" my grandmother replied. Then, as if she'd heard what Mama said for the first time, Grandy turned to her and asked, in a fierce whisper, "You mean to tell me you eat from that *nasty-dirty* woman? You mean to tell me you put the food she give you into your mouth?"

"What make her nasty, Ma' Louise?" Mama was really angry now. "Her dishes always well clean, she carry herself neat and tidy. Her house even cleaner than mine! What make her so nasty?"

"You know what I mean." Grandy lowered her voice so I wouldn't hear what she was saying. "*All them mens.*"

"She combed Gloria's hair, ironed her uniform, and got her off to school for me for two whole weeks. That's all I care about!"

"*Still,*" Grandy insisted, "she's not the type of person you should be associating with. *You have Gloria to think about!* You have to set an example for your daughter!" They both looked over at me, sitting at the table by the window, fiddling with my home-work, pretending not to be listening to what they were saying, though they knew full-well I was listening to every word that

12

came out of their mouths, and they both ended the conversation. Once I was outside the house the argument would begin again.

I loved Rachel. It was not only that she helped us out when Mama was sick; even before that she always had a kind word or a fruit for me. She smiled at me at the standpipe and always put me in front of her when we were in line to catch water. I knew a lot of sailor-men came to visit her when their ship was in on Thursday evenings, that everyone talked bad about her because of this, but that didn't matter to me. As far as I was concerned, people in the yard were just jealous of Rachel because of the pretty things she had in her house. Her bed was always made up with a silk and lace bedspread from abroad; her floor was polished a bright red colour, and there were the flowers, the plastic flowers of many different colours she bought in the flea market downtown and arranged over her bed, around her dresser, in the cracks in the walls. And there were the postcards, lots and lots of postcards, from the sailor-men after they'd gone back home.

Whenever she got a new postcard Rachel would call me over to read what it said. I would carefully pronounce every word, telling her exactly what was written. Sometimes, when something in the card was to her liking, Rachel would laugh out loud and ask me to read again what her suitor had said. She'd then say it over and over to herself as if committing it to memory. She listened carefully to every word that passed my lips and if the tone of the letter changed, she abruptly ended the letter-reading session, saying we were getting into big-people-things and she would ask one of her big-people-friends down at the wharf to read the rest for her. She never failed to compliment me on my reading and encourage me to continue doing well in school. A kind of sadness would come over her then, and one day she said to me, "Yes, if there's one thing I would encourage any young woman to do, it's to do well in school."

"Yes!" Mama waved the newspaper at Rachel, "Gloria pass her common entrance for All Saints High School!"

"Well this is good news!" Rachel passed her eyes briefly over the newspaper before turning to flash me a big broad smile. "Is no surprise to me you passed your examination, Gloria, for everybody know you're a very bright little girl. Still, this is well done, well done of you!" and she took her hand out from under the sheet and handed me a navel orange before pulling me into her arms.

I loved going into Rachel's sweet-smelling arms almost as much as into my mother's. I would lay my head against Rachel's chest and listen for the steady, even beating of her heart, as I sometimes did with my mother. Just the sound of her heart pounding steadily away gave me the most comfortable feeling in the world.

"You must be the only child in this yard who pass her common entrance examination. Everybody will be jealous of you, but most especially Miss Christie who believes her Denise is the brightest and best thing around town, although we all know differently. There is reason to celebrate today, if not too loudly. Gloria, you did well. You did very, very well." She wrapped her arms so tight around me the many gold bangles she wore jingled loudly.

"But you don't think..." my mother stopped, "you don't think nobody would try to do *anything* to Gloria?"

By "anything" she meant – would someone put an awful curse on me so I would die a frighteningly horrible death before I even started attending All Saint's High School? Would I suddenly get an itch, scratch it, and have the itch turn into a sore that would never heal? I could see the thoughts racing around my mother's head. After all, her face seemed to say, bad-minded-people put a curse on her father when he came back to Jamaica from Panama with all of his Colon money – and look what had happened to him. The young-green-man had fallen down dead one day, for no reason. No reason at all. Bad-minded-people.

"I tired telling you," Rachel said, exasperated, "obeah only catch you if you believe in it."

Mama shook her head from side to side. "No," she said softly. "Obeah can catch anybody. Even those who don't believe in it ..." Before Rachel could utter another word Mama was in the kitchen, rummaging around for a lime to cut and sprinkle around the room.

Later that day I was the talk of my primary school and my class teacher took me to the principal's office. The principal leaned back into his swivel leather chair behind a large desk, and smiled at my teacher. Framed certificates hung on the walls – all the schools he had attended in England and Canada.

"Well, well, well," he said, leaning over his desk and reaching out a hand to me, " if it isn't my little spelling bee champion. And today, Gloria you've put our school on the map again, so to speak. You've made us proud." The *Gleaner* was spread out on his desk and my name and the name of the school circled in red. I was the only student from the school to pass the common entrance examination.

My teacher gently pushed me forward. All morning long she repeated how bright I was to the other teachers who came to the classroom wanting to meet me; she had known I would pass. She had been keeping her eyes on me, and this was no-surprise, no-surprise-to-her at-all!

The principal cleared his throat and sat back in his chair. "I wish I had more students like you in this school, Gloria," he was looking out the door to the playground. It was recess and children were tumbling over each other, playing on the jungle-gym in the yard. When we got back to the class it would be all about who'd lost a ribbon, or who'd broken a brown bandeau an aunt in America had sent for her. Looking out at the playing field it suddenly hit me with a tremendous force that I was leaving this school where I'd spent the last nine years of my life. I knew all its secret hiding places: where the sixth grade boys took the sixth grade girls to push them up against the walls and feel under their blouses (not even the Principal knew where that was!); the battered old water fountain where it was rumoured ground lizards lived; and in the middle of the school, the garden where students grew large smooth eggplants no one ever ate ( I could never understand why we grew them in the first place). Suddenly my future loomed large, dark and uncertain in front of me.

In my new school I would be wearing a four-pleated box skirt and a cream-coloured blouse edged in burgundy – not the navy blue tunic and white blouse I had worn all my life. I would not be free to pick and choose whichever shoes I felt like wearing, but would be required to wear dark brown shoes with dark brown socks every day. And there would be all those students I did not know. Students from preparatory schools. A bubble started forming in my throat that kept growing larger and larger. My eyes began to sting and burn. Before long, the walls of the principal's office dissolved in tears. Already change had begun to set in. This morning as I'd walked into class, an eerie silence settled over the entire room. I didn't know what to make of the silence. Were my classmates happy for me? Were they sad for themselves? I made to walk over to the group of girls who'd been my friends for the past six years, but they closed the circle and left me standing outside of it. One of the girls, Raphaelita, a girl who had stayed at my house when her parents first left for New York, whispered, loud enough for me to hear, "And I guess she thinks she's all *that*!"

The group broke into laughter.

"I'll be going to New York soon, anyway," Raphaelita bragged, "and I don't need to go to any stupid high school in Jamaica!"

I turned from Raphaelita to Natasha to Nicole, but they all screwed up their faces, letting me know I was no longer welcome in the group. The tears came and I started fumbling in my pocket for the handkerchief I usually carried, but it wasn't there. I was making such a mess of everything.

"Come now, Gloria," the principal said, coming from behind his desk and putting a heavy arm around my shoulders, "this is a day of celebration, not tears. You can always come back to visit us, you know." He handed me his handkerchief. "In fact, I insist on it. Promise me you'll come back to see us. Right, Miss English?" he said, looking over at my teacher and winking.

Looking at the principal through the heavy curtain of my tears, I suddenly did not care if he was really a rum-head as most people said he was, that he could be found singing loudly in bars all over Kingston every Friday night after he got paid. I didn't care if Miss English acted more English than the *real* English people did, pretending she couldn't speak or understand a word of plain Jamaican patois. I was suddenly ashamed of the times I joined in the laughter and made fun of the way she walked, her two knees knocking against each other. None of this mattered any more.

When I got a hold of my crying the principal handed me a brown paper bag. Inside were three books: two Nancy Drew mysteries (my absolute favourites!), and a book by someone I did not know, an H.G. De Lisser, who, the principal said, was from Jamaica. I took the books out of the bag and ran my hands over the hard covers, tracing the spines. In my mind I could see the words tumbling over each other, swift like the river near Grandy's house after a hard shower of rain. I would read each book twice. They would become part of my personal stash. I would never lend them out.

"Thank you so much," I finally managed to say and smiled up at the principal.

"You're very welcome!"

It was the end of April. Before long I would be off, spending my summer holidays with my grandmother in the country. Sophie, Monique, Junie and that girl Yvette were all there. Plus there was Nilda and Denise in my yard. Who needed the girls at school anyway?

Three women were standing outside the yard, talking, as I walked home from school that evening: Miss Christie, Nadia Blue, and Miss Sarah.

Miss Christie lived in one of the cottages in the back of the yard near the standpipe with her daughter Denise who'd just had a baby. Five years ago when Miss Christie moved into the yard, everyone wondered who this yellow-skinned green-eyed woman with her red-skinned hazel-eyed daughter was. It was obvious she came from some kind of class and standing. Gradually the story came out and Mama's sympathy was rewarded with a performance.

Miss Christie had disgraced her Upper St. Andrew family when she got pregnant by a married man, a well-known business-man much older than Miss Christie who made sure both she and their daughter were well taken care of. While he was alive, Miss Christie lived in an apartment in New Kingston with helpers to take care of their every need – Denise attended one of the island's best preparatory schools.

During this time Miss Christie kept pressing the man to leave his wife; to marry her. "Karl, I can't stand this life I leading any more! You and I both know you no longer love the old witch you call a wife – if you ever did. So why don't you leave her? Why don't you just pack up your things and move in with us?"

"In time," Karl kept promising. But the man never left his wife, and after a while Miss Christie got used to him staying with her a couple nights and going home the other nights. Over the years there were many terrible fights with the wife who accused Miss Christie of being a home-wrecker, of flaunting in her face the many things Karl bought her. Worst was the time the wife found out where she lived and turned up at the apartment in New Kingston.

"You will never get him!" The wife flung at the closed door, all the neighbours looking out. "If you think you'll ever get him, you're dreaming some kind of dream."

The wife was a tiny Chinese woman, no more than five feet tall, and Miss Christie had been surprised how loud her voice could be. She'd let the woman carry on outside her door for as long as she could, hoping she would get tired and go away, but after a while she saw that if she wanted the woman to leave, she'd have to shame her in front of the people gathered outside.

"I have him more than you do!" The wife brandished her gold wedding band. "What you got to show for yourself? If you had any decency, any decency at all, you would let this married man alone and his children!"

"I got this apartment to show!" Miss Christie replied triumphantly. "I have this apartment, the car outside, all the furniture I could possibly want and a bank book full of money!"

"You think so eh?" The wife was frothing at the mouth. "Well, I will show you who have this apartment! I will show you who have the car outside! I will show you who really own the furniture inside of that house! As for the bank book full of money!"

The wife was close to tears. She could not believe Karl was doing this to her. Her father had *made* Karl, had given him everything he now had, and this was how he had chosen to repay her? When she first brought him home, her family nearly had a heart attack. A black man. Lin had brought home a black man. And not even a nice brown-skin black man, but one as black as midnight. They tried talking her out of it. Asked her to con-sider-the-consequences-of-her-actions. The "confusion" of any children. The-difficulty-of-fitting-in. But Lin turned out to be more stubborn than even they knew. Stuck by Karl, bore him five strong boys (whom the grandparents now adored), and her parents had given Karl the money he needed to start his now-flourishing business and this was how Karl had decided to repay her? Karl would be sorry. So very sorry.

Miss Christie was not prepared for what happened next. In fact, she hinted late one night to my mother, when they were both sitting outside on the verandah and talking, it was down right suspicious. For the strapping healthy man just keeled over one day in his office and died. Not even one month later. His secretary came in and found him with some green thing coming out of his mouth.

"*Just like that?*" my mother asked, incredulous.

"Just like that," Miss Christie replied softly.

Again the wife showed up at the house. The pale freckled hand with its gold wedding band up against the window. Karl had made no provision for Miss Christie or for Denise in his will. In fact, there was no will, and the apartment and the car were in her husband's name. As for the furniture and the bank-book-full-of-money, *that* Miss Christie could keep, for *that* would go so quickly from a woman who only knew how to work on her back. The wife stood guard at the door with six police officers as Miss Christie was forced to move out of the apartment. This was how she eventually ended up in the yard. Miss Christie was crying by the time she finished telling my mother the story, and my mother was quiet for a long time, no doubt recalling a similar incident with my own father. Mama reached over and took Miss Christie's hand.

"It happens to the best of us," she said, sighing. "At least you knew there was a wife. Some of us didn't even have that luxury." They said nothing else the rest of the night, and I don't know how long they stayed out there like that, because, after a while I stopped my eavesdropping and fell asleep.

Everyone expected my mother and Miss Christie to become firm friends since they were the only two women in the yard to have gone to high school, but this friendship never came to fruition. For one thing, Miss Christie was always in some kind of competition with my mother, always trying to one-up Mama in conversations. She kept insisting she knew more about every-thing than anyone else in the yard. After all, she had travelled abroad a few times, thanks to Denise's father. To make matters worse, Miss Christie had taken an instant and total dislike to me, because of how bright people said I was.

When I was younger my mother sometimes left me with Miss Christie when she went to work. Miss Christie took away my lunch and put me to stand in a corner for the stupidest reasons.

"You might be a little princess for your mother," Miss Christie would say, "but you are not any princess for me!"

If she happened to be watching several other children, Miss Christie would organize a reading or spelling contest. It always came down to a race between myself and Denise, who, truthfully, always seemed bored with these contests. I always ended up winning, much to Miss Christie's dismay and once she left me standing under the tamarind tree where red ants bit me all over my legs, causing them to swell up badly. By the time my mother came home my legs were so swollen they looked like two tree trunks. That night, when my mother asked me what happened, I told her everything Miss Christie had ever done to me in my life, and my mother stormed out of the house and gave Miss Christie a good cursing out! That was the end of their blossoming friendship.

The other woman, Nadia Blue, lived at the front of the yard, across from the mad woman who collected bottles and cans on her daily trips around the city and hung them on the shrubs growing wild in front of her house. Nadia lived with her man, Jesus, and their five children. Jesus and Nadia were forever quarrelling and fighting because of all the other women Jesus had. It seemed every few months someone was either pregnant or just had a baby for Jesus.

Jesus' dream was to make it to America, to New York, where he would make so much money he could live like all the foreigners and drug dealers who flocked to the island during the Christmas holidays. Jesus would buy a car; no, more like a whole fleet of cars with the money flowing like milk and honey on the streets of New York. He would drive around in style and be treated like the don he really was. He would take care of Nadia and all his other baby mothers. Nadia wouldn't have to take in other people's clothing and scrub and wash them until her back ached and her fingers were pale and wrinkled from constantly being in the water; the children would have everything they needed. He would lavish special attention on Nadia, for even though he had several other baby mothers, Nadia was his main woman. She was the one he worked the hardest to get, they'd been together the longest, and they'd been through the most together.

"I don't care how pretty a woman thinks she is," Jesus was fond of saying, "she can never come before my Nadia. Nothing in the world can ever separate us, for no matter what, my Nadia not leaving!"

And he was right about that; for all they quarrelled and fought, Nadia would never leave Jesus. She had been with him from the time she was sixteen years old when she'd moved out of her mother's house just to be with him.

The last woman was Miss Sarah who lived in the yard before it was a yard, had lived there when the place was open land where stray goats pastured. She was an old woman with thinning gray hair, but still surprisingly sprightly for her age. She knew everybody's business: which young girl was pregnant even before she started to crave green mangoes with salt, and who the girl was pregnant for even when she was trying to keep the man's name quiet. She had a daughter in England who regularly sent her money and kept promising to visit but never seemed to make it. It was rumoured that Miss Sarah had this daughter with a sailor-man, that in times gone by she had been no different from Rachel, but Miss Sarah vehemently denied this. Her daughter's father, she always insisted, was a respectable white gentleman with whom she'd lived for several years. When they broke up, he took the child back with him to England.

"Good evening Miss Sarah, Miss Christie, Nadia."

"Well, well, well, if it isn't the little bright spark who passed her examination," Miss Sarah said. "I stayed clear round the back and heard your mother this morning."

"What school you pass your examination for?" Miss Christie wanted to know.

"All Saints," I mumbled. Miss Christie always made me nervous and uncomfortable.

"Oh," she could barely conceal her surprise.

"That is good, really, really good," Nadia started smiling down at me. "I hope one of my girls will get into a good school like that. Perhaps Nilda will go to a school like that. She didn't pass this time, but there's always next year ..."

Miss Sarah began shaking her head in amazement when she heard the school I was to go to. "You so bright! So very bright!" I could hear the affection in her voice.

"These girl children," Miss Christie sighed heavily, "they can be such a disappointment. Such a disappointment. If Denise had been studying her books instead of studying how to get a baby I am sure she would be going to that school today. But they are such a disappointment these girl children, and you can never tell what will eventually become of them, even when they start out young and full of promise."

Miss Sarah took the chewing stick she was munching on from her mouth and sent a stream of white spittle flying out in front of her.

"Stop all this right now, Miss Christie! Your Denise was always too force-ripe for her age. And everybody know she not nearly as bright as our Gloria here. I have no qualms about saying Gloria is the brightest child in this yard, maybe even the brightest child around these parts. And she well-behaved and mannersable too, even if we don't like some of the friends she keeps." Miss Sarah winked at me and the other two women started laughing. Miss Sarah reached down in the pocket of her housedress, pulled out a bill and handed it to me.

"I've been waiting to give you this all day. Give the money to your mother to put in your piggy-bank for you. She pass here not too long ago with a bag of pig tails and red beans, so I know she cooking stew peas and rice for dinner tonight!"

Immediately I was hungry. Stew peas and rice was one of my favourite meals. One I hadn't had in a long time.

"Thanks for the money, Miss Sarah," I said, walking away.

"It's nothing at all. Nothing at all. You a good child."

"And you must come and help Nilda when her time come to take the exam again next year," Nadia Blue said after me.

Not a word came out of Miss Christie's mouth.

As I approached our house the smell of pigtails drifted out into the yard and enveloped me. I could make out the thyme, pimento

22

and escallion Mama put in the stew. I stepped into the house and Mama smiled over at me from the tiny kitchen.

"Guess what? Mean old Rutherford let me out early today so I could come home and make a special dinner for you. He said congratulations to you on passing your exam, old cruff that he is."

For the first time in a long time, Mama looked young, happy and carefree. She was wearing a T-shirt and a pair of faded denim shorts and had a big cooking fork in her hand. Her hair was not up in a severe bun as it usually was, but down around her shoulders. There was an unmistakable sparkle in her eyes.

"Come here!" She called me over to the pot, as if she had a big surprise on the stove. I pretended Miss Sarah had said nothing to me and feigned surprised when I saw the tiny white dumplings floating up over the pink pigtails and red kidney beans.

"That's not all," Mama continued, seeing the look on my face. "I'm making soursop juice sweetened with condensed milk and nutmeg just the way you like it. Change out of your uniform and help me set the table. Put on the white tablecloth with the gold-flowered embroidery. Tonight we celebrating!" She blew me a kiss before turning back to the pot.

Usually I grumbled whenever I was given additional chores, but not today. I put down my school bag, took off my school clothes, and started doing what my mother had asked me to do. Yes, tonight we were celebrating!

## CHAPTER 2

Grandy came a few weeks later, bearing gifts as usual. This time it was star-apples, june-plums and sugar cane. Whenever she came, Grandy brought all the fruits in season and I always hurried home from school when I knew she was there. Today, as I came into the yard, I spotted her sitting on the verandah, almost hidden by the hibiscus tree, rocking in the rocking chair. She was eating a piece of sugar cane and fanning herself, and her face broke into a huge smile when she saw me.

I stood for a moment just looking at her. Mama and Grandy looked so much alike! Same high wide forehead and bushy "Indian" eyebrows. The only difference between the two was their weight: Grandy was much heavier than Mama, with an ample bosom I secretly believed was made for me to rest my head on. I made a mad dash for the verandah and stood before her.

"Just you look this bright girl that pass her common entrance examination!" Grandy said, eyeing me. "Just you look this bright girl that going to All Saints High School! Come now and give your old Grandy a kiss."

She pulled me down into her lap and I buried my face in the side of her neck and the chair rocked harder as she laughed and laughed. Grandy had a smell all of her own. A kind of fresh country smell, doused in rosewater. Grandy handed me a piece of sugarcane from the plate beside her. The emerald streaks through its dull yellow colour gave promise of just how sweet the cane would be. I bit into it and my mouth immediately filled with the sweet juice.

"I just can't believe it! You getting so big and all! Now you off to high school when it seems like only yesterday I was at Jubilee

24

Hospital looking down at you curled up on your pink baby blanket. Such a tiny little thing you were, we had to pin you down on the blanket so the wind wouldn't blow you away. A-baby-no-bigger-than-the-palm-of-my-hand. Now you're getting ready for high school of all things!"

"Grandy," I nuzzled even further in the side of her neck, "you forever telling me that story!"

"Well, it's God's own truth! I'm not lying! It does seem that way to me! Getting ready for high school!"

"Not before I spend my summer holidays with you!" I said, knowing how much this would please her. Later, when I asked her for money to buy tamarind balls and lollipops, *and* begged her to carry the dress my mother had bought but was refusing to allow me to take with me, I knew from experience she would agree to at least one of my requests.

"You little trickster!" she pushed me roughly away from her. "Think I don't know what you're doing? No tamarind balls for you today!"

"Me, Grandy?" I gave her my most big-eyed, innocent look.

"Yes, you! You're the biggest trickster of them all! Worse than Anansi ownself! If Anansi could trick everyone and get two plantains to eat, you could do the same thing and get four!"

I lowered my eyes feigning shame.

"Ginnal!" she handed me another piece of sugarcane.

We sat together, quiet for a little while, both of us eating sugar cane. I was still on her lap and she kept rocking in the chair.

My summer holidays would begin next morning when I set off with Grandy to Lluidas Vale, the tiny village deep in the dark-blue mountains of Portland. It was where my grandfather, Grandy's sister, Aunt Clara, and Grandy's mother and father, none of whom I'd ever known, were all buried. It was where my mother had been born and had grown up, and where I spent every summer holiday.

"You finish packing the clothes to take with you?" Grandy wanted to know.

"I've almost finished packing," I told her.

"Almost not good enough," she gave me a push and smiled. When she smiled, folds of dark brown skin crinkled around

25

her dark brown eyes, and it was almost as if, beneath her skin, several different peoples were warring to assert themselves, but no one was quite winning.

"We have to make sure you're done packing tonight, for we leaving first thing tomorrow morning."

I smiled and said nothing. Every year there was a tug-of-war between my mother and me as to which clothes I'd take with me to the country. All my shorts would go, because I would be outside most of the time and it was the hottest time of the year. I would take the one yellow bath-suit I'd had for years – getting too tight for me, I thought, but not as far as my mother was concerned. All my old jeans and T-shirts – my yard clothes – would go, for I needed those to wear about the place. But what I most wanted to take was the sheer pink dress Mama had bought two weeks ago for my graduation from primary school. But she'd spent good money on the dress and I wasn't to take it out of the plastic bag it was hanging in, much less consider taking it to the country with me.

Last night, when I thought Mama wasn't looking, I'd taken the dress out and kept looking and looking it over. It had garnered oohs and ahs at the graduation. Many people wanted to take my picture. The sheer material shimmered in the lights, and the large bow at the back, with what looked like fish-scales, changed colours depending on how the light hit it. Quite a stir that dress caused. Easily the prettiest dress in the entire place.

And now Mama wasn't allowing me to take the dress with me to the country, because *I didn't know how to take care of anything*, was always *ruining the things she used her hard-earned money to buy*. Every year she complained Grandy didn't supervise me enough, allowing me to have my own way, running all over the place like some wild animal, staining-up and dirtying-up all my good things. Every year when I came back home she'd say all I had in my bags were rags and she couldn't believe Grandy was the same woman who had grown her, who would breath fire on her when *she* was growing up if she got so much as a spot on her clothes; here she was so lax with me now.

"Just what do you think you're doing with that dress?" Mama demanded when she caught me with the dress on my lap. "Gloria, don't you realize you're getting to be a young lady now? That it's time you started taking more care of your things? Tell me, Gloria, you really think I have the money to be buying back the things you ruin over the summer?"

I stood there, pretending to be listening to her, but what I was really doing was singing a little song in my head to drown out her ever-present voice.

"You need to take more care of your things! You need to become more responsible! Take Nilda for example. She is your age, yet the two of you are light years apart in behaviour. If Nadia is not home, Nilda takes care of herself and the younger ones, as good as her mother! Nilda don't dirty-up her good clothes, she can even wash her own clothes! Why can't you be more like Nilda?"

This was always her question to me. Nilda this, Nilda that, why couldn't I be more like Nilda? Meantime I kept trying to figure out how I could take the earrings with the tiny ruby and emerald bird – as well as the dress. The earrings with the dress! Now that would show Junie, Sophie, Monique, and especially that girl Yvette, who was boss! I really wanted Yvette to see the dress, for she, more than any of the other girls, was always running her mouth that nothing I brought from Kingston was anything new. Nothing special. Nothing she hadn't seen before.

"Mama," I said, committing the crime of interrupting her, "Can I just please take the dress with me to the country? *Just please*? I promise to take extra good care of it!"

She looked at me as if I was crazy. "No," she said with finality, "you cannot take the dress with you."

I'd stood there just looking at her. Why didn't my sad face move her? I never seemed to get away with anything with my mother. It was then I decided what I would do. I even convinced myself it was Mama's fault that I had to resort to my plan. After all, I'd asked her up front to take the dress and she'd refused. Now she was forcing me to get Grandy to take the dress for me.

My mother was still talking as I schemed. "By the time you come back home that dress will be fit only for the garbage! Mango stain, guinep stain, all sorts of stain will be on that dress."

Grandy always said if Mama had more children, or if she had a man to come home to in the evening, then these *little things* would never bother her so much.

27

"She only fuss so much with you because you're the only one. She focus all her attentions on you. It wouldn't be the same if she had other people in the house…"

Sometimes I *did* wish Mama had something or someone else to attract her attention, especially when I wanted to go outside and play and she refused to let me. But in truth, I really could not see Mama with a man or with any more children. I could not see Mama with anyone but myself. There were the times when she took my face in her hands and just stared and stared down at me. She would straighten out my eyebrows and kiss me on the tip of my nose and I knew I was the centre of her universe.

"I can see everyone in your face," she would say. "I can see Mama, Aunt Clara, I can even see your father…" she always paused when she mentioned that-man-your-father, "his bones, his eyes, the set of his face. When you turn sideways I can really see your father. But not only him. Many different people in our family I can see in your face."

Mama rarely spoke about my father and, the few times she did, always hesitated before talking about him. Mostly she spoke about him only when she was upset about something I had done, or the difficulties she was having in raising me by herself. Then she talked about how my father had abandoned his responsibility and left her alone to raise me.

"Lying, conniving wretch!" she would always begin. "I wonder if he even still with that so-called wife of his! The years of my life I wasted with that man! Lying, conniving wretch!" This would usually suffice for a few months – until she added something else to what seemed to me an unending list of all the bad things my father had done to her.

"A man," my grandmother was always saying. "Your mother needs herself a good man. Someone to come home to in the evenings. Someone, other than you, Gloria, to fuss and bother herself over. You can't yet understand it, Gloria, and I can't begin to explain right now the difference a good man can make to a woman's life. All I can tell you is things would be very different if your mother had herself a nice gentleman-friend."

And Grandy was always on the lookout for a man for Mama. Every time she came to visit she would tell Mama which one of her "schoolmates" in Lluidas Vale was still single, and which one asked after her lately. If Grandy was there when a man she considered eligible was visiting Mama, she would go out of her way to try to make the person feel more comfortable, and always ended up doing just the opposite. Grandy would heap praises on Mama, about how well she could cook, how neat and tidy she was, how kind-hearted and giving. Grandy continued like this until Mama excused herself from her guest, and called Grandy into the back room. A hushed quarrel would follow.

"Stop it! Just stop it!" Mama would whisper. "It's not what you think! He's just a friend."

"Friends make the best husbands," Grandy would reply, loudly enough for the visitor to hear.

"For Christ almighty's sake," Mama would say, "stop it! It's nothing like that. I tell you, he's just a friend."

"All right!" Grandy lowered her voice in defeated anger. "I just hope one of these days someone other than your "friend" walk through that door!"

Mama would go back to her visitor on the verandah, and Grandy would sit down inside seething. If Grandy happened to look over at me, she would start on what a disappointment my father had been; she was sorry the day my mother ever set eyes on that-man-your-father. She would say all of this very loudly, as if she'd forgotten Mama had a visitor on the verandah.

"Rotten good-for-nothing scoundrel. Mash up my daughter life. Give my daughter a child and run away and leave her to deal with it alone. This was never the life my child was meant to live." Grandy's eyes would cloud over and fill with tears. Her chest would heave, she would reach into her bosom for a handkerchief, look around the two tiny, crowded rooms Mama and I called home and shake her head.

"Not that I have anything against you, Gloria," she'd say when she saw tears gathering in the corners of my eyes. "You know I love you more than life itself, for you is my own flesh and blood, and somehow we always manage to love our own flesh and blood. But your father, Gloria, your father – I cannot lie, I cannot stand the man!"

I remembered him vaguely. My father. When I was younger he

29

would visit on Sundays, sit me on his lap, and try to talk and play with me, but everything was so stilted, so out of step, he would just give up. He was someone who wandered in and out of my life, and expected me to be cheerful whenever he was around. Then there was the bothersome change in my mother when he visited. She seemed to lose her voice and could not speak. He had to keep asking her to repeat everything she said. Worst of all was the fact that she always seemed to be trying to get rid of me when my father was around, sending me out to play in the yard, (something she did not ordinarily do), telling me to go visit one of the women in the yard (again, something she did not ordinarily do).

If my father happened to stay for dinner, my mother took down her best plates for him to eat on, gave him the biggest and best pieces of meat and piled on layers and layers of rice and peas, potato salad and lettuce and tomato until he had to tell her to stop. He would look down in embarrassment at the huge mounds of food on his plate – although he always managed to eat everything up and sniff around for more. If my mother happened to look at me at meal times during his visits, it was always with a look of disapproval at the many rice grains scattered around my plate. I, of course, always made sure there were lots of rice grains scattered around my plate to keep my mother's eyes busy.

These visits came to an end one Sunday afternoon when a woman turned up in the yard looking for Mama. She arrived just after my father left and had obviously followed him. Mama and this woman ended up in a terrible fight. This woman told Mama she was my father's wife, that they lived together in Vineyard Town with their four legitimate children, and why didn't my mother and her bastard-child leave her husband alone!

My mother almost died from the shock of it all. My father had told her he lived with his parents, strict Christians, in their home on Red Hills Road, and as soon as he got his own place, we would all be living together. The one good thing that came from the incident was the friendship between my mother and Rachel. For while everyone else in the yard gathered around the two women, spoiling for a fight, Rachel had sense enough to realize Mama had never fought a day in her life. When the woman pulled out a long silver butcher's knife out of her bag and started brandishing it in my mother's face, she didn't know what to do. She just stood there, mouth open, looking at the woman. I started crying loudly and Rachel pushed through the cheering crowd and grabbed the woman by her neck as if she was nothing but a peel-neck fowl she was about to skin.

"Listen to me, and listen to me good. You cannot just walk into this yard where this woman live, pulling knife against her and expecting to get away with that." The crowd stopped their cheering and quieted down, and you could tell some of the people were beginning to feel ashamed of themselves.

"Now I want you to get out of this yard before *I* have to do something to *you*. Make sure you through the gate and up the street by the time I count to three. One …"

"Tell her to leave my husband alone!" the woman said, struggling in Rachel's arms.

"No," Rachel said, through her teeth, "*you* tell *your* husband to leave *her* alone. Two .."

Looking around her, at all the faces now turning sour, the woman dropped the butcher's knife in the dirt and fled. I never saw her again. And I never saw my father again.

But just now there was the problem of the pink dress. Yes, I would get Grandy to take the dress. Another tug-of-war would begin. For Mama was convinced Grandy was spoiling me, and Grandy was convinced Mama didn't know what she was doing. Mama often reminded Grandy I was *her* child and *she* had given birth to me. Grandy would laugh and say she had given birth to Mama in the first place.

"Why, for example," Grandy wanted to know, "you have this child bathing in cold water in the mornings, I will never understand. Don't you know she can catch chronic in her bones and die? Don't you know you should warm the water for her to bathe in?"

"Warm water!" Mama would point to the small gas stove in the kitchen. "If she need warm water, she can warm it herself! There is the kettle! There is the stove!"

"Nonsense!" Grandy would reply. "Is something you should do for her. It was something I used to do for you, even when you were a big girl, big enough to go get yourself pregnant! Come

Gloria," Grandy would say, "I warmed this water for you. Come let me give you a bath."

Grandy started by pouring the hot water from the kettle into the plastic basin in the bathroom. Then she added cold water, testing the water with the tip of her finger until it was just the right temperature. She then dropped a piece of bluing into the basin and watched it spread through the water, until it was the colour of the deepest parts of the ocean.

"Step in," she would say softly.

"She not a baby, you know!" Mama would shout. "You only put bluing in the water when you trying to keep ghosts off of babies and Gloria not a baby any more!"

"Don't pay any attention to her," Grandy would say. We were now two half-circles coming together to form a perfect whole.

Once I was in the water Grandy began by soaping my rag into a creamy lather, then started washing down my back, my arms and chest, my legs, my fingers and toes, inside and outside of my ears. "Stand up," she would say, and, very gently, she would wash between my legs. Often as she did this part, Grandy talked to me in a hushed voice, telling me all sorts of fanciful tales.

When she was done giving me a bath, Grandy told me to stick out my tongue. She examined it, and my teeth, rubbing my tongue with a clean rag. When she was satisfied everything was as it should be, she wrapped me up in a towel and held me in her arms. Mama's eyes would roll up to the sky.

Yes, I would let Grandy take the dress. By the time I came back home Mama would be so happy to see me she would forgive whatever I'd done to the dress. And, I *would* take extra good care of the dress so as not to get any stains on it.

I got up and followed Grandy into the house, changed out of my school clothes and came back out on the verandah with two star-apples. Before long Nilda came over and sat down beside me.

"Here," I offered her a star-apple, but she shook her head. Something was bothering her. It seemed lately something was always bothering Nilda.

"They're at it again," she said quietly.

"What for this time?" I could just hear Nadia's and Jesus' voices rising in their house.

32

"The usual." Nilda was using her toes to toy with a piece of dried leaf at her feet. After a while she stopped doing this and let her head hang down in front of her. "Aren't you happy you don't have a father, Gloria? Aren't you happy you don't always have to deal with all that arguing? That you can have peace and quiet in your house? Aren't you happy about that?" She sounded so hopeless I didn't know what to say.

"No, you don't want one, believe me. You don't want a father. You don't want that cussing and fighting every day. Believe me, you definitely don't want that."

Both Jesus' and Nadia's voices kept getting louder and louder. Everyone could tell a fight was brewing and a small crowd was forming outside their door. Furniture was being shoved back and forth and curses were flying.

"I'm tired of this life ... all those women!" Nadia was shouting.

Grandy, who was preparing dinner inside, came to the door with an onion in her hand. She listened for a while, shook her head and went back in the house.

"Another one ... another one pregnant for you ... and you can't even feed the ones you already have! Look at this place ... look at how we living, Jesus!" There was silence for a while before Nadia spoke again. "Where you think you going? Why you putting on those clothes? I'm talking to you! Talk to me, Jesus!"

There was the sound of cloth tearing and bodies tumbling around inside the house. Nadia cried out in pain and Jesus came running out, his shirt in shreds. Nadia was close behind him with a pot of water. She threw it at him, but he dodged and ran through the gate. Her eyes were red and her bottom lip was swollen. She must have fallen and burst her lip because Jesus would never hit her. He had many faults, Jesus, but hitting women was not one of them.

"What?" she looked out at the crowd and got even more upset. "You never see a man and woman fuss in all your lives? What you all staring at?" The crowd started to disperse. She looked over to Nilda, and the sight of the girl's misery must have enraged her even more. "Nilda," she shouted, "get your tail into this house right now."

Nilda rose without saying a word and went to her mother. I

watched her go and realized there was a heaviness about her that hadn't been there before. I would have to try and talk to her one of these days, that girl Nilda.

"I can't believe they're still living like that," Grandy said, coming out on the verandah again. "All these years and they're still cussing and fighting? Man is trouble own self you know, Gloria. You would never believe all the trouble man can get you into. Lie, lie, lie. Nothing lie like man. And as changeable as star-apple leaf! Why they can't stay with only one woman, God alone knows! Now that you're going to high school and have your whole future in front of you, you have to stay far away from them. They can blighted your future!" Her eyes moved quickly over my thin frame, stripping me of my clothes, looking beneath my skin, past my bones all the way down into my body to see if it had started to mature, to see if my body had started to betray me. Not finding any evidence of what she was looking for, she looked relieved.

"Well, anyway," Grandy said, "you still a little girl. We still have time to work on you."

I wasn't sure what it meant – them working on me – but I knew it had something to do with becoming a woman. I did not know what made one a woman, I only knew that becoming one was very dangerous. Something to lead one astray. I only had to look at the women around me. The way something about their bodies had betrayed them. Rachel. Nadia. My mother. This woman thing involved something, I concluded long ago, easily lost and almost impossible to regain. I was glad I was not yet a woman. Was far, far, in fact, from becoming one – though if anyone asked me what made one a woman, I would not know what to say.

I got up and followed Grandy into the house. I went over to where the pink dress was hanging and took it out of the plastic bag knowing my grandmother would look over and see it.

"Oh!" Grandy said when she saw the dress, a gleam coming into her eyes. " Now, isn't that a beauty." She came over and took the dress and felt its material. "Such a beauty. Oh, what a beauty is this sheer pink dress!"

## CHAPTER 3

I knew Yvette was going to be a problem from the start. She stood at the top of the hill, looked down into the glistening river and dared us all to get naked.

"Naked? You must be *crazy*, Yvette! Grandy would kill me if she knew I was up to some foolishness like that!" Yvette was proving to be her usual difficult self. All the time I'd been sitting in Kingston and dreaming of coming to the country to see her – to see them all – I couldn't believe I'd forgotten this side of her, the side that was always testing, pushing and challenging; the side that always needed to be in control.

She threw herself down on the grassy banking. "Well," she said very loudly, "I guess some people are not as brave as they make themselves out to be. I thought some people from Kingston would do just about *anything*."

"That *anything* doesn't include getting naked so some stupid country boy can walk by and see me. What do you all say?" I turned to the other girls, seeking support.

Sophie looked down intently at something by her toes. Junie was suddenly very interested in some bush close by. Monique as always wanted a compromise.

"Well," she said, turning to Yvette, "do we have to take off *all* our clothes?"

"All of them!" Yvette replied, waving her arms about like some mad magician.

The sun was strong overhead and I was hot. Too hot for all of this nonsense. I'd already been in the country for two weeks and this was my first visit to the river. I couldn't wait to get into the cool river water and wade in up to my knees. I'd scoop some of the water up in my hands and let it fall all over my hot and tired face. Yvette with her foolishness was keeping me from that water. Of course, I *could* have gone in without her, and I knew that chances were the other girls would follow me in, but I didn't want to do this. Yvette might get upset and take off, and much as she got on my nerves sometimes, I did not want that. The outing just wouldn't be the same without her, difficult as she could be.

When I'd told Grandy I was going to the river with my friends to catch shrimps, she stopped frying the plantains for breakfast and thought about it for a moment.

"Well," she looked in the direction of the mountains, "don't look like we going to get any rain today so I guess it's alright for you to go." She gave me a wide-top tightly woven reed basket she used to catch shrimps. After telling me I should set the basket on the far side of the banking, where it was cool and dark and where the shrimp congregated, she warned me about the river.

"Now you know that river has a mind of its own," Grandy was buttoning up the back of my dress. "If it seems unruly, don't go .: If your mind tell you not to go in, follow your mind. Should it start raining - the river starts rising, get out fast!"

Grandy and all her insu .. ions! It seemed my entire existence was hedged around what I should and should not do; what I should be leery of: Spirits were in the bushes; I should not throw a stone at a bird, especially if it was a very pretty bird or a black black bird because it might not be a bird at all but some spirit in animal form; I should never answer a first call but listen for my name on two or three more calls, for it might not be a person calling me at all but a ghost pretending to be a human and appearing in human form and this ghost would take me back with her to her grave and no one would ever see me again; and, under no circumstances, should I take shelter under a silk cotton "duppy" tree.

"Pure foolishness," Yvette said when I told her about this as we walked to the river. The sun was so hot, we often had to seek shade under a tree. I was on the look out to make sure it was not a silk cotton tree, much to Yvette's annoyance. Like Rachel, she had no patience whatsoever for anything she considered superstitious.

36

"I don't know about that," Junie whispered fearfully. "Before I was born spirits killed my younger brother and my father's mother. I'd be careful if I were you."

Monique and Sophie grunted their approval.

"*Diarrhea* killed your brother and *heart attack* your grandmother! Not spirits and bushes and duppy foolishness!"

"And how you know that, Miss Know-it-all Yvette?" Junie jumped to her feet, ready to fight. Junie was a good fighter, in some ways a better fighter than Yvette, despite Yvette's mouth. "And just what was it that took *your* mother away?"

A fearful silence descended over the group. What would Yvette say or do? A shadow darkened Yvette's face and her bottom lip began to tremble. For a moment it seemed she was about to cry, and if she started crying I didn't know what we'd do. Yvette could be "hard" at times, yes, but she also spent hours and hours, crying for no immediate reason. Her mother had left for New York over three years ago and since then no one heard anything from her. Not a word. Not a letter. Nothing. No one knew if she had landed, if she had not landed, or if the plane had just been gobbled up by the infamous Bermuda triangle. Yvette's mother simply disappeared in thin air it seemed, and the people in the district often openly speculated if she was even still alive. Sometimes I looked at Yvette, wondering how she did it, how she survived day after day, month after month without getting any information about her mother? As miserable as my mother could sometimes be, as miserable as she sometimes made me, I knew I wouldn't be able to cope with people openly speculating whether she was alive or dead. I knew I could not live without my mother.

Yvette's face darkened some more, but this time in anger. A sneer spread across her full dark lips and I could tell she was getting ready to say something really hurtful.

"Well," she said to Junie, "if you or your mother could read, you'd know what it said on the death certificates."

The joke about Junie and her mother was that even if their names were on johnny cakes in front of them, they wouldn't know it, for neither could read. This was not exactly true. Junie wasn't the brightest girl, but she could read a word here and there, a few sentences. She certainly knew how to spell her name, fill out forms. True, she wasn't as bright as Yvette, but then few people were. Had Yvette taken the common entrance exam, she'd surely have passed for one of the high schools in Kingston, but she hadn't taken the exam because her father couldn't find her birth certificate and there was no way to verify she was of the age to sit the exam. What would become of her when she finished primary school, no one knew.

"Can't read? Says who?" Junie asked, her hurt showing, ready to fight.

"Says me and everybody else." Yvette's arms were akimbo, daring Junie to touch her.

"I have a good mind to punch your stinking mouth!" Junie doubled up her fists and started getting closer and closer to Yvette. "That would teach you to keep it blasted shut!"

"Just you try it!" Yvette was trying not to show she was afraid Junie might make good on her promise. "Just you try it!"

"Alright, alright, that's enough!" I stepped in to calm things down between the two young lionesses with fire breathing out of their nostrils. Junie and Yvette eyed each other, smelling and circling each other for quite some time...

Now as we looked down towards the river, I thought if we didn't do something to please Yvette we'd have a miserable time. I realized if we stayed near the rushes, it wouldn't matter much if we took our clothes off, for no one could see us from way up here on the road. There were certainly enough bushes and trees sloping down to the river to hide us. It wouldn't be the first time we'd stripped down naked in front of each other; we'd done that dozens, perhaps hundreds of times before when we came to the river. But now that our bodies were changing ...

"Look, we'll take off as much of our clothes as we're comfortable with."

"Coward!" Yvette mumbled under her breath.

"Will you just shut up! Will you just for once keep your big mouth shut?" I was getting really angry now. "Do we want to go to the river or don't we?"

"Let's go," Monique said, jumping up and getting ready to lead the way.

"Let's go under the bridge," Yvette said in yet another dare. The girl was seriously getting on my last nerve! The bridge was the place Grandy had warned me time and time again not to go near. The water under the bridge was dark and it was deep. There you could not see the bottom of the river. There were sharp stones hidden in the water under the bridge, and because it was so dark it wasn't easy to see them. Someone could really hurt themselves on those stones. This was what the district people said all the time. People had to be careful with those stones. But that was not the worst of it. Under the bridge was ole crab and rivermumma! Yvette herself knew that. Another terrible hush fell over the group.

"Are we going or not?" Yvette was looking around her, something lit and burning bright inside her, something which looked like the bright orange-red flowers of the poinciana trees. Flame of the forest, those trees were called. As bright as any midnight fire. I looked at Yvette. She had already accused me of being a coward for refusing to take my clothes off; now I could not refuse her dare without looking even more of a coward in front of the other girls. I would give in. We would go under the bridge. I was the Kingstonian. I was the one supposedly afraid of nothing.

"Sure, we can go under the bridge," I said, struggling to sound brave.

"Well, all right then," she said, triumph in her eyes, "Let's go. Let's go under the bridge!"

We started climbing down the banking, which was rocky and steep. Trees sloped down to the river forming a heavy green canopy overhead – cocoa trees, banana trees, breadfruit and a few mango trees. When they were in season, the district boys would raid them, picking all the ripe fruits, leaving the trees as bare as the backside of a newborn baby. We stayed close to the ground, clinging onto bushes, baskets under our arms, as we gingerly made our way down. Yvette was in front, followed by Sophie, Monique, Junie and finally me.

Water rushed swiftly and thundered over the falls a little way ahead. The sound was very loud, because there was quite a drop, and the water seemed to growl going down, releasing an ever-present puff of white spray as if it were the breath of some dragon.

Grandy often told me the story of the man coming home drunk one night who tumbled down the slope and over the falls. It took days to find his mangled body. The river gets hungry for companionship every now and again, Grandy said, opens its mouth wide to take someone in. Even the youngest child knew enough to be wary of the falls. This was why we always went upstream, towards the bridge.

Before long we left the trees behind and were out in the hot sunshine again. We reached the water's edge. We hitched up our skirts above our knees and wedged the baskets carefully under our arms. Beads of sweat had formed on Yvette's upper lip and I watched as she lifted her skirt to wipe the sweat off her face. Her chest was heaving from the effort of climbing down the mountainside.

"So," Yvette drawled, jolting me out of my thoughts, "why you staring at me like that?"

"And what are you using to know that I'm looking at you?"

Sophie and Monique giggled, while Junie shook her head.

Yvette hissed her teeth and began wading out into the shimmering silver pool of water where it looked like someone had thrown many golden sparkles. Her clothes started to cling to her slender frame and I could not help thinking how beautiful she was. She was one of the darkest persons I knew and certainly the most striking with her hair combed into four thick plaits. Beside her, Sophie, Junie and Monique seemed like wilted hibiscus flowers. Her mother, whom I had never seen, was still talked of as a beauty, so much so people were wary of her. You could never trust so much beauty. People said this was her downfall; why, young as she had been, she was "kidnapped" by Yvette's father. I continued looking at the girl, who suddenly turned and flashed me a smile. I looked away quickly, but all the other girls began to laugh.

Before long we were crossing over to the other side of the river to set our baskets for the shrimps in the cool dark rushes.

I was the last to step into the water and I jumped back onto the banking for I had forgotten how ice-cold it was. Every year I forgot that. I took a deep breath and stepped in again. This time I stood for a while in the water without moving, letting my ankles grow accustomed to the chill, watching the tiny green and black groupers darting around my feet, before I started wading out, the water coming up to my ankles, my knees, then my waist and finally my shoulders. I was now holding my basket overhead like the other girls, swaying every now and again in the strong pull of the current, my dress clinging, pasting itself onto my body. I spotted some bright yellow guavas bobbing by on their way down stream, dropped from a guava tree at the side of the river, and if my hands had not been holding the basket, I would have made a dash for them.

The other girls reached the other side of the river near the tall green reeds, and were busy setting their baskets.

"What's taking you so long?" Monique called, laughing at me. I was still making my way gingerly over to them. The others did not need to say it with their mouths for I could see it in their eyes: *Watch the Kingstonian who knows everything; the Kingstonian who is having such a hard time crossing the river.*

"I'm coming, I'm coming!" I yelled.

"Just make it this year," Monique yelled back and everyone started laughing.

I made my way over to the reeds and set my basket, then followed the other girls who were now heading upstream to the bridge. Under the bridge, it was a relief to take off our dresses, clinging and cold, an unnecessary weight on our bodies. Junie unbuttoned my dress and I pulled it over my head. But I would not be taking off my panties, wet as they were. It was one thing to be naked with my friends in the privacy of my grandmother's house where we took showers together, a totally different thing to be naked at the river where a complete stranger could come by. Without discussing it, all five of us kept our panties on.

Under the bridge was cool, damp and dark. Slimy green moss was everywhere. We all knew how deep the water was just by its stillness. If Grandy knew I was there, I'd get a fine beating. Every year there was some new story to tell. *Did you hear what happened under the bridge the other day?* Grandy, like other villagers, spoke of the water under the bridge as if it had a mind of its own.

There were cement platforms on which you could sit or stand, but these were covered with some kind of thick waxy green plant. I refused to even think about what might be hiding in there just waiting to crawl out. Then there was the huge crab living under the bridge for years and years. Every now and again, it was said, someone caught a glimpse of this crab crawling out of his hole, claws as big as a child's arm. Grown men had supposedly lost toes, fingers, eyes or even had their stomachs gauged out by this crab. What would this monster do to us?

And what of the dreadful rivermumma? What would *she* do to us? Rivermumma loved children. Especially girls. And here were five of us to drag down to her watery kingdom; five new attendants to comb her long green hair and sing with her at night, luring other little girls to their deaths. I did not care who might want to laugh, I was not getting into that still dark water. The bridge started to tremble and for a moment I was confused. Was this retribution for disobeying my grandmother? My legs went weak and my breath came fast. My fear must have shown on my face because the other girls started laughing.

"Is only a vehicle passing," Monique said.

"I guess you think that's funny?" I was not seeing the joke.

"Verrrry funny," Yvette replied, wrapping her arms around herself and falling backwards into the water. For a moment she disappeared under the dark surface, before emerging near the far end of the bridge. She drew my eyes to the bank behind her, where red ginger plants grew in abandon, their large clumsy banana-like leaves tearing easily in the wind. Beyond was a dense thicket of trees and bushes, home of the notorious sasabonsam, hairy monster with large blood-red eyes, sitting high in the trees dangling his long hairy legs, ready to catch whoever dared come into the bushes. Suppose sasabonsam came tearing out of those bushes right now? Just what would we do? Another shiver ran through my body.

Monique, Sophie and Junie squealed and jumped into the water, one after the other. They started doing powerful breaststrokes, sometimes diving under the water, or lazing on their backs.

"Come on, Gloria," Sophie said. "Don't be a chicken. Come in!"

"Yes," Monique and Junie chimed in, "the water feels soooo good."

"Last time I was in, it was soooo cold."

"That's until you get used to it!" Yvette joined in. She dived, emerging next to the other girls. All four of them treading water, looking up at me.

"Oh come on," Junie begged, "the water's real nice. You've no idea what you're missing."

"Look at this!" Yvette shouted. She dived and we saw her two skinny legs shoot up in the air. She remained like that for a split second before disappearing into the water. She re-emerged sputtering and laughing.

"You found it again!" Sophie shouted. "I can't believe it! You always find the stone first!"

The stone was in the middle of the river and very difficult to find. It, too, was legendary, for it wasn't unusual for someone to spend an entire day under the bridge and not find the stone. Like ole crab and rivermumma, the stone was said to appear only to those it wanted to stand on it. Now all the girls crowded onto the stone, held hands and started singing and shouting at the top of their voices. Every so often one or other of them would fall off the stone, because it was not large enough to hold four people.

"Let's play a ring game," Monique suggested.

"Yes!" Yvette agreed, arms flailing about. "A ring game! Let's play a ring game!" She was having the time of her life.

"Which one? Which one?" Junie asked, equally excited. Anyone looking on would not have believed they were the same two girls who almost came to blows a moment before.

"Stagolee!" Sophie shouted. "I am Stagolee!"

The others chimed in: "Stagolee stole the cookie from the cookie jar."

"Who me?" Sophie asked, bracing back and pointing a finger at herself and looking at the other girls.

"Yes, you!" they shouted back, in joy.

"Couldn't be," Sophie said, shaking her head and shoulders from side to side, denying the theft.

"Then who?"

"Number four," Sophie said pointing and laughing at Yvette, "stole the cookie from the cookie jar."

"Who me?" Yvette asked, pointing a finger back at herself and shaking her head.

43

"Yes you!"

"Couldn't be!"

"Then who?"

"Number one stole the cookie from the cookie jar."

With all the singing and rocking they were doing, the circle broke apart and they all went under the water, before coming up and joining hands in a circle again. The more I looked at them, the more fun they seemed to be having. I put my toe in the water and twirled it around, watching circles spread into larger circles in the water. I put one foot in up to my ankle and left it there. The water really did not feel that cold; perhaps I would go in after all.

"Come in! Come in!" they chorused when they noticed what I was doing.

Next I was sitting with both legs dangling in the water. I pushed off from the cement block and the water enveloped me. This time it felt warm and silky, like Grandy's loose warm hugs and kisses. The girls made a place for me and I joined the circle in the river. Soon I was singing at the top of my lungs with them, our voices echoing loudly under the bridge.

"Seeee," Yvette stuck out her tongue at me; "there was nothing to be afraid of!"

Nothing at all I agreed. Not Grandy; not ole crab; not sasabonsam, and certainly not rivermumma. How could she handle five girls all at once? The circle broke apart and we dived under the water, emerged, took air, blew bubbles, splashed water at each other. We felt we'd never had such a good time.

"Let's check our baskets," I suggested when we had been in the water for more than an hour. "They must have a lot of shrimps by now." They agreed and we dived under the water and emerged at the far end of the bridge. It was only when we were out from under the bridge that I remembered we were almost naked. I wanted to turn back for our dresses, but the others disagreed, saying we should just check our baskets and get back quickly under the bridge. There didn't seem to be anyone around to see us.

We waded over to our baskets; they were filling up rapidly with silver-gray shrimps. Later when we got home, we would poach them over an open fire and watch them turn a brilliant red. We would salt and pepper them and eat them with roasted breadfruit or boiled green bananas. The baskets checked, we hurried back under the bridge.

"What game shall we play now?" I asked.

"What about Mango Time?" Sophie suggested.

"That's not a game, stupid," Yvette said. "That's a song." We continued holding onto each other on the rock. By now our fingers were pale and wrinkled from being in the water so long.

"You've got breasts!" I said to Yvette, looking at the small mounds on her chest.

"And you too!" Yvette pointed back to me.

"Just barely." There was just the barest hint of a rise on my chest.

"I have nothing!" Monique muttered, gathering up the skin on her flat chest.

"You know what's going to come next," Yvette said solemnly.

"*It!!!!*" we all said, letting out a shrieking cry.

"I don't want *it* to happen to me," Monique's eyebrows crinkled up. "Everything will change. Plus, I just don't understand certain things. Like, you know, can you still pee when *it* happens? And does *it* come all the time, non-stop?"

Not one of us could answer her questions. Neither Mama nor Grandy ever spoke to me directly about *it*. I only knew one day *it* would happen to me and after that, if I were not careful with boys, I could get pregnant. *It*, I knew, involved blood, and often times women were miserable and tired because of *it* and felt a lot of pain. *It* called for sanitary napkins, and sanitary napkins could be troublesome and expensive. Why did women have to have *it* in the first place? It was something all the women I knew wondered. After a while *it* went away and women could not become pregnant any more. All this information I had picked up along the way, since no one really sat me down and talked to me directly about *it*. Like so many other things in my life, innuendoes were supposed to suffice for direct information and somehow I was just supposed to know all these things.

Suddenly I heard bush breaking as if someone was coming towards the bridge from the hill. I stopped playing and listened intently. It might be a stray animal, in which case the sound would take no particular path, would move about from place to place, in

45

a straggly fashion, but these sounds were different. Sure in their step and heading straight for the bridge.

"What's that?" I asked, raising my hand to still the talking about me. For a moment everyone went quiet.

"What's what?" Yvette asked, slightly annoyed, as if I were making things up.

"That!" I said again, panicking, for the sounds were getting louder. It was coming in our direction. Then we all heard it. Someone *was* coming towards the bridge.

"Good lord," I groaned, my mind running all over the place. If it was Grandy I was dead. If it was sansabonsam, I was dead. If it was some stupid country boy... that thought I couldn't follow to its logical conclusion. We began swimming vigorously towards the cement blocks. When we got there it was pure confusion. I could not find my dress, while Monique, Junie and Sophie were struggling over the same dress. The only one who remained in the water was Yvette. She didn't seem the least bit concerned that someone or something was coming, and acted as though she didn't have a care in the world. She continued treading water, stopping every now and again to stand on the stone in the middle of the river. Every once in a while she turned in the direction of the bushes to see who or what might be coming out.

Three boys appeared at the far end of the bridge. Three boys from the district. Immediately they started laughing and pointing at us. "Look at them! They naked! We see you naked!" This was terrible. No boy had ever seen me naked or near-naked before, and I had promised myself that none ever would. Here now were three boys staring at me in my underwear. Three country boys to boot! I would never live down the shame.

"Look! Monique in her panties!" one of the boys said, doubling over and laughing hard.

I could not get the dress over my head fast enough. I kept getting lost in its folds, struggling for what seemed an eternity. Finally Monique, Sophie and Junie were able to sort out their dresses and pulled them on. I managed to do the same.

The boys acted as though this was the funniest thing they'd ever seen. From the looks on their faces, they evidently thought they had something over us. Something they could use to bribe us, because we wouldn't want anyone else to hear about this little incident.

"You dirty disgusting boys!" Monique screamed at them. "Go away! Go on, get away from here." Her arms were akimbo. Now that we were dressed again, we found our voices and were ready to fight.

All this time Yvette remained in the water unconcerned, watching what was going on around her. She wouldn't be cowed by anyone, least of all these three boys. She had come under the bridge to enjoy herself and this was exactly what she was going to do. Swaying and rocking in the water, in her own little world.

"We were up in the mountains bird hunting when we heard someone under the bridge." This was Jingles, one of the boys, laughing so hard he had to struggle to catch his breath. "I figured it would be my brother and his friends down here. I couldn't believe it when I seen you girls checking your baskets. You girls sure have gumption to be playing under the bridge!"

If only we hadn't gone to check the stupid baskets!

"Yvette," one of the other boys started taunting her, "why don't you come out of the water?" He was mocking her, teasing her, acting as if he had some kind of power over her. He believed his mere presence could make her stay in the river for as long as he wanted. How wrong he was.

"I wish you would all just get lost!" Monique shouted again, trying to get them to leave.

"You want me to come out of the water?" Yvette asked in a calm clear voice.

"Yes!" The boy said, still believing he had the upper hand.

"OK, I will." Yvette started slipping out of her panty. "I will give you just what you came for. Exactly what you came for!"

I could not believe what I was seeing. Was Yvette really slipping out of her panty? A frightful and eerie silence descended over everyone. I knew Yvette could be daring, but this was over and above anything I knew. The boys all got quiet and seemed afraid of what Yvette was doing

We continued watching in stupefied fascination as Yvette sent her panty adrift down the river. Now things were really getting out of control and the boys started to retreat. Then, Yvette did a stunning flip on the stone and both her slender dark legs shot right up from the water. She balanced herself on the stone in the middle of the river for a split second, before falling back in the water. She had done the flip facing the boys completely naked.

Everyone went absolutely quiet. We did not know what to do with ourselves. We all knew Yvette was brave – brash even – constantly pushing against some invisible rule or the other, but none of us thought she would go this far. In that moment we all knew Yvette had done something powerful and unsettling, but we didn't know what it was. The boys began a hasty retreat. Yvette had taken whatever power they'd thought they had in pouncing upon us, frightening us and seeing us naked, and she'd turned this upon them. Now I knew for sure they would keep their mouths shut.

After she had made her stunning flip Yvette remained under water. We were all suspended in an uneasy bubble. It was as if what had happened was so bright, so terrific and amazing we were all momentarily blinded by an over-bright light. No one said anything; we all just kept looking at the water.

"Yvette?" Junie called out suddenly, breaking the spell. "Lord Jesus, where is Yvette?" Junie asked, panic in her voice. "Yvette should have come up by now."

"Looook!" Monique screamed, pointing to the middle of the river.

Yvette was just below the surface, face down, in the water. My stomach flip-flopped.

Junie was the first to find her voice. "Let's get her out of the water." All four of us jumped back in and started struggling to get hold of Yvette. When we did, my stomach contracted violently: blood was pouring out of a huge gash on her head. In her flip, she must've hit her head on the stone in the water. She was so still my legs went weak. I felt as if the energy was pouring out of me as fast as the blood was pouring out of the gash on Yvette's head. We started trying to haul her back to the cement blocks. What we would do with her there, I did not know. Then I spotted a shocked Jingles watching us, remorse creeping over his face. The other two boys had disappeared.

"Take her arms," Junie said to Monique and me. "Sophie and

I'll try to get her legs." We pushed and pulled at Yvette until somehow we managed to get her to the cement banking.

"You," Junie said, pointing at Jingles who was now trembling badly, "go and tell Mr. Robinson to come with his van, quick! Tell Aunt Lilly to come too. Bring a large towel. We need a nurse. Go now, quick!"

The boy seemed to have been waiting for an order and took off immediately

"We need something to stop the bleeding." Junie was looking from Yvette to the bushes on the banking. "Gloria, come give me a hand."

I could not move. My fingers and toes felt as if they were made of lead, and my tongue was so dry and heavy in my mouth I could not get any words out. I was no use to anyone at all.

"Gloria!" Junie screamed, "give me a hand!" She was shaking me, but I could only stand there looking down at Yvette.

"Well, stay there," she finished angrily, and turned back to Yvette who was much too still. Junie pulled at the hem of Yvette's dress, and the hem gave after a couple of pulls. She folded the cloth into a thick pad, knelt over Yvette and put it over the wound. We watched to see if that would stop the bleeding. It did not. Soon the blood started soaking through the cloth.

"Sophie," Junie's voice was forceful, "hold the cloth on Yvette's forehead while I get something to stop the bleeding." As soon as Sophie had taken the bloody pad, Junie jumped back into the water and started making her way over to the bank.

I wanted to tell her to stay out of the water, that it was the stone in the middle of the river that had done this to Yvette, but I could not let out so much as a small croak of protest.

I watched helplessly as Junie climbed out of the river and started searching the bushes. She was looking for something; what I did not know. Perhaps she was using her grandmother's bush-woman eyes. I watched as she pulled close to a particular bush, smelt it, then moved away shaking her head. Finally she found a bush, broke it, smelt it, and was satisfied. She began pulling off leaves in fistfuls. When she had enough, she ran back down the bank and carefully waded back to where we were. She crushed the leaves in her hands until they were soft and pliable,

49

lifted Yvette's head onto her lap and started covering the wound with the crushed green leaves, all the while chanting unfamiliar words. Soon the bleeding started to slow and I could tell whatever Junie was doing was working. Monique, who'd kept quiet all this time, suddenly started to shake uncontrollably and cry.

"Yvette," Junie cooed softly to the lifeless body in her arms, "any moment now Aunt Lilly will be with us. Hold on; just you hold on."

Everything seemed to be in slow motion. I only hoped Jingles had enough sense to get help along the way, because we sure needed help right now. Junie still had Yvette's head in her lap, and was putting more leaves on the wound. Yvette's blood was all over her, but at least the bleeding continued slowing down.

After what seemed like ages, I heard voices in the distance.

"How many times must we tell these children to stay away from the bridge!" one woman was saying, and from the sound of her voice I could tell she was hurrying. "But no! These children don't listen to us. Now look what happen, that Yvette gone and hurt herself!" an awful fear was gnawing the woman's voice.

"There is Mr. Robinson coming with the car now!" a man shouted. Three women and two men started coming down the hillside towards us. Everybody looked as though they'd dropped what they were doing and come running. The men were in their water-boots and the women in their aprons.

"Lord Jesus have mercy!" one woman cried, when she saw Yvette's limp body and the blood all over Junie.

"Jesus, Jesus, help us!" another woman raised her hands up to the sky.

Taking off shoes and water boots, rolling up dresses and pants around their legs, these five adults waded out into the water. Aunt Lilly, to our great relief, was among them. As soon as she reached Yvette, Aunt Lilly bent and took her wrist, checking for a pulse. The look on her face made my knees go even weaker.

"We have to hurry! We have to get her to the hospital." She took up some of the leaves still on Yvette's face and smelled them.

"Who crush these leaves and put it on her face?" she asked, astonished.

Very softly, Junie said, "It was me."

"If this girl lives any at all, it's because of you."

Junie looked down and said nothing.

"Come," Aunt Lilly said to the two men, "let's get this child to the hospital."

They wrapped Yvette in the towel they had brought and the two men lifted her and started across the river with her, up the bank and then the long haul up the hill, Aunt Lilly close behind them.

"Look, Ma Louise's granddaughter there," someone said, pointing at me still standing on the concrete slab under the bridge. "She's shaking like a leaf. Lets take her home; let's take them all home."

Grandy was hanging clothes on the line when she saw me with the group of people coming towards her. She dropped the clean white clothes she was holding in the dirt and ran towards me, fright all over her face.

"Jesus, God, you all right, Gloria?" She took me in her arms, feeling me all over to make sure everything was still in place. "Gloria, talk to me and tell me you all right? Why she not talking to me?" She pressed her hands over my face, around my neck and down my arms as if she was checking to make sure I was really there in front of her.

"What happened? What happened to her? Where the other girls? They all right?" She fired off questions, one after another. "The river ... Lord my Jesus, I can't find the words ... nothing not making any sense."

"It's all right, Ma Louise," one of the women said; "this one's all right; it's the other one we have to worry about. She not looking too good at all."

"Yvette, she hit her head bad on the stone under the bridge. Mr. Robinson taking her to hospital in Bay, right now. Nurse Lilly gone with them. She not looking too good at all."

Grandy's eyes bulged. "Yvette? Yvette?"

Yes, the people around us nodded.

Grandy looked down at me. She'd warned me not to go under the bridge, but that didn't matter right now. All that mattered was

51

I was alright and another child was hurt. She pulled me into her arms and I buried my face in her chest and sobbed. She held me close and let me cry. "It's alright," she kept saying, "you safe, it's all right. Everything will be all right now."

Grandy and I visited Yvette in the hospital a few weeks later. She had a thick white bandage around her head and still suffered from terrible headaches. She greeted both Grandy and I heartily however, and ate all the oranges and bananas we brought for her. There was a constant stream of visitors, we were told, and almost everyone who came to visit brought Yvette food.

"Before she leaves here," the Nurse wagged her fingers playfully at Yvette, "she will be one plump little girl!"

Yvette remembered nothing of the accident. She remembered everything up until the boys came, but everything after that was blank. She knew something terrible had happened to her, but she had no details. Neither Grandy nor I had any desire to fill her in and kept quiet. It had taken me days to be able to talk about what happened, and I still could not tell the story without breaking down, crying and shaking uncontrollably. Every night since the accident I had the same dream: a chocolate-skinned woman with moss-green hair was stretching out her arms to embrace Yvette and offering to take her back with her to her watery kingdom at the bottom of the river. When Yvette refused, the woman got angry and decided to take her whether she wanted to go or not. What ensued was a fight between this woman and Yvette, a fight Yvette only narrowly won.

"Rivermumma." Grandy sighed when I told her the dream. "All you girls have to stay far away from that river, for rivermumma, she has her eyes on you."

As if anyone had to tell Sophie, Monique, Junie or I never to set foot in that river again!

Yvette asked after the others, "especially that dunce Junie." She said this laughing, for she had been told Junie had saved her life.

"Junie is just fine. Getting ready, like everybody else, for the big Independence Day celebrations."

"Is she now?" Yvette was laughing.

"Yes she is and you know it!" I poked her side.

Apart from Christmas, Independence Day was the biggest celebration on the island and I could hardly wait for the day to come. There would be music, dancing, food and all kinds of festivities. I hoped this year the junkanoo man would show up again and do his little dance. We never knew which year he was coming, the junkanoo man, or if he was coming at all, so his presence was always a delightful surprise. He would show up wearing a cow mask with two huge horns hiding his face, and a long black tail sticking up in the air from his monkey suit. He would appear, as if out of nowhere, in the centre of the festivities, and he would dance. Oh, how he would dance, for hours at a time, sweat streaming down behind the cow mask. He would do the most elaborate and fancy footwork, and do it so well it seemed he was floating above the ground. Then he would dance around the crowd, the scent of rum on his breath, collecting whatever anyone decided to give him, before he took off again, blending into the bushes, disappearing as imperceptibly as he had come.

"Too bad you're going to miss it," I said softly, because I knew how much Yvette loved the celebrations and how much fun we'd had last year.

Yvette shrugged, as if Independence Day didn't matter to her, but I knew differently. I was a little sad. Independence Day always marked the end of my summer holidays; shortly after that I went back to Kingston to start the new school year. I leaned close to Yvette and whispered, "The pans are out. The ones they jerk the pork and chicken on!" I knew how much she loved jerk pork and chicken.

Again she shrugged as if this didn't matter.

"That chicken. That pork," I continued, smacking my lips at the imagined taste. Grandy looked down at me, frowned and shoved me.

"All right," Yvette conceded, "save a piece of jerk pork for me."

"Will do," I replied, smiling at this girl with whom I had the most bizarre of friendships.

On Independence Day Grandy started her usual sermonizing about the ways of these-latter-days-young-people.

"Instead of going to Church and praising the Lord for letting them live to see another Independence Day," Grandy said, huffily, "they will be there in that dark dance hall tonight rubbing up against each other and sinning themselves. I wonder if they even know what they celebrating?"

"As if it's not something you used to do!" Uncle Silas-Nathaniel smiled at Grandy, easing off his water-boots at the door before coming into the house. Uncle Silas-Nathaniel was Grandy's "friend" who stopped by on his way to and from his field every day. He had breakfast and dinner at Grandy's house and she took him his lunch in the fields. Since Grandy was a churchgoing woman and since her church sisters had already brought her up before the Pastor because of this "friendship", Uncle Nathaniel was never allowed to stay too late in our house, especially not after dark, although there were times they both pretended they didn't know what time it was and Uncle Silas stayed as late as he wanted. When he stayed late, they'd sit on the verandah, so that the bushes with eyes to see and ears to hear could see and hear exactly what they were doing. When he thought I wasn't looking, Uncle Nathaniel reached over and pinched Grandy on her bottom. Grandy swung around quickly to chastise him with a dish-towel, but I could see from the look on her face she was delighted with what he'd done and was only pretending to be upset.

"Emma-Louise," Uncle Silas-Nathaniel was saying in that playful way of his, "I remember when every night you used to be in the dance hall swinging your hips and dancing late into the night! You was one bad dancing girl!"

"You're one wicked, wicked liar, Silas Nathaniel Thompson!" Grandy said, turning to her pot to hide the colour rising in her face.

"You telling me?" Uncle Nathaniel was laughing. "I might be old, but I sure not senile. Not yet anyway. I used to watch you, even way back then. You had the smallest waist of all those other girls; and boy, did you know how to move that wire-waist of yours!" They were so very fond of each other, Grandy and Uncle Silas-Nathaniel. Every year Uncle Silas asked Grandy to marry him, promised her the sun, the moon and the stars up above, but every year Grandy declined. Marriage would be too much of an entanglement for her old age; she had been married once before

54

and would only ever be married to one man in her life and that man was buried in the Lluidas Vale graveyard, had been buried there for years.

"I don't know what you talking about!" This time Grandy's voice was lower, less sure. "I don't remember ever setting foot in that dance hall."

"No, not *that* one, but one just like it. Think hard, I'm sure you'll remember."

Grandy started peeling green bananas furiously and dropping them into the pot of boiling water on the fire. Uncle Nathaniel always knew exactly what to say to get Grandy flustered.

He came close behind her in the kitchen, Uncle Silas Nathaniel did, and I pretended to be even more interested in the book in my lap.

When he was very close behind her, Grandy said in a very stern voice, without turning around to look at him, "Just you remember the child is here."

Uncle Silas Nathaniel looked at me and came over to where I was sitting. "What you reading?"

"The White Witch of Rosehall." It was one of the books the principal from my old school had given to me.

"Oh," he started rubbing his hands together, "now that's a good ghost story. A good-good duppy story! You know I like me a good duppy story!"

Uncle Nathaniel was always telling me stories. Ole crab, sasabonsam and rivermumma. He told me about a golden table, which rises every noon in one of the rivers on the island, just for a split-second, before descending back into the waters. Many people had spent their entire lives chasing the golden table, and still no one was able to get it out of the river. Legend had it that the golden table was created during slavery times by a greedy pirate who sank clutching it to the bottom of the river. Uncle Silas told me about women who could shed their skin at night and assume whatever shape they wanted, and about a white woman who floated around on a three-legged horse. The night before he'd told me about the dreaded rolling calf.

"It's the spirit of a butcher who come back riding one of the cows he killed during his lifetime. The dead cow have fire for eyes and snort smoke through its nose. The butcher sometimes drag a heavy chain behind him, or, he lasso the chain around in the air with a whooping cry, just like this," he was moving his right hand around and around in a circle in the air. "If you ever see such a thing, run, Gloria, run!"

We were sitting on the verandah and night was thickening around us. Grandy was busy sewing. I pulled closer to Uncle Silas. In my mind's eyes I could see the fire-breathing monster coming out of the darkness and charging straight at us. Grandy looked up and saw that I was afraid. "Why you always telling the child those silly things eh, Silas? You want to give her nightmare or something? You can't think of anything better to tell her?"

"But she need to know these things!" he protested. "If she don't know these things, what will she do if she ever come face to face with a rolling calf? How will she know to make her way to the first four-road junction and lie down like a star so the rolling calf can't pass her?"

"She's a Kingstonian and you know there's no duppies and rolling calf in Kingston."

"Says who? You think the duppies draw some line between Kingston and everywhere else? It's just because they have so many street lights in Kingston why the people there can't see all the duppies walking around. For if there's one place where duppies sure to be, is in Kingston! All the murders in that place! All the duppies that must be walking around!" Uncle Silas paused after saying this. Minivans were being stopped, people forced to undress and robbed in the middle of the day. One boy had walked into a classroom and shot another boy dead in front of the teacher. Yes, all sorts of terrible things were happening in Kingston.

"Those drug dealers," Uncle Silas was saying now, "those damn deportees. They are the ones causing all this problem on the island... Police shoot-outs with all kinds of gunmen. Little children getting killed in their yards and on their verandahs. All those things happening in Kingston."

Around where I lived men lazed on the street every day, nobody working, but everyone, it seemed to Mama, Rachel and Miss Christie, had lots and lots of money to spend. There were the local dons, the ones who made a name for themselves because of how many people they were rumoured to have killed. These men were especially frightening because they could have just about any woman they wanted, whether she wanted to be with them or not. Mama was afraid of the men on the corners and would walk with her head down, praying no one would say anything to her. Rachel, though, nobody would bother – probably one of the other reasons why Rachel and Mama were such good friends.

Uncle Silas was hoping to get a response out of Grandy about the crime and violence, spreading like ink on paper, all over the island, but Grandy kept her head down, paying attention only to the sewing she had in front of her. Kingston was far away, a place she only visited every few months. She made sure she prayed every night that nothing would happen to me or to my mother.

When Uncle Silas saw that Grandy was not paying him any attention, he descended into a brooding silence. Then, as if to lighten things up, he looked over at me and said, "I mean, Gloria, who wouldn't want to have the field that I have? And the girl that I have?" He was teasing Grandy to get her attention and it worked. She put down her sewing and stared at him, a smile beginning to form on her lips.

"What is it you want this dark-dark night?" Grandy asked Uncle Silas, smiling. "Why you bothering me tonight of all nights?"

"So you stop that sewing of yours and pay some attention to me and your granddaughter here. You know she going back home soon, and day and night you will talk about how you so miss her!"

"OK," Grandy said, laughing, "you have what you want: you and my granddaughter there have my full attention."

"And that is all that I ever wanted," Uncle Silas told Grandy. "All I ever wanted."

Grandy looked at him for a long time before she looked at me. "Tomorrow, first thing, go to Merlene and get your hair cane-rowed for the Independence Day celebrations. That pink dress," she winked at me, "you going to wear it tomorrow. And those gold earrings your mother gave to you for passing your examinations, you make sure you wear those earrings tomorrow too. For it might be," she laughed when she said this, "the last time you get to wear those earrings. Think how upset your mother must be that you took them!"

"But it wasn't I who took them," I protested, "it was you!"

She looked at me, shook her head and smiled.

Often times I accompanied Grandy to visit Uncle Silas in his field. He would take me by the hand, showing me his prized cucumbers, scotch-bonnet peppers and plump ripe "plummy" tomatoes. He would use his chin to point at a pumpkin still on the vine, for everybody knew that if you pointed directly at a pumpkin with your fingers, the pumpkin would dry up and fall off. Schoolchildren in China knew that. He showed me his prickly pale-green cho-chos and would pull fat orange carrots from the dirt for me to see just how big they could grow.

Like my grandfather whom I never knew, Uncle Silas had spent years in Panama as a young man working on the canal. Colon was where he made the money he used to buy his land. He and Grandy must have been "friends" even back then, for he often spoke about how abruptly my grandmother's letters ended, and how, when he came back from Panama to marry her, he found Grandy had tired of waiting on him, married my grandfather and had my mother.

I never knew my "real" grandfather because he died when my mother was no more than a few years old. When Grandy spoke about him a mist would come over her eyes and she would get very sad. She would talk about how much fun he'd been, that-man-Ralph-Adolphus-Prescott, how he courted her by throwing love-bush on trees around her yard and daring the bushes to grow. When the bright orange love-bush took over the hedge, forming clouds and clouds of stringy orange blossoms, he presented himself to her mother asking for Grandy's hand in marriage; the ever-growing love-bush made him know how much my grandmother already loved him.

Grandy's voice often cracked when she talked about how, after he returned from Panama with his money, he took sick under suspicious-suspicious circumstances. No matter what she did, however many doctors and bush doctors, preachers, pastors and herbalists she took him to, he did not get better, and the young-green-man died, just like that, bright and early one Sunday morning. Died right there in her arms. Some evil was behind it, Grandy always insisted, but she left the evil doers to God, for she was not going to dirty her hands and her heart by trying to get back at wicked people. Her husband was now with God and she would see him again one day.

"Hi Emma-Louise there!" one of Grandy's church-sisters called out as we came onto the streets for the Independence Day celebrations. "I see you decide to come out and stretch your legs after all."

"Might as well. Nothing else to do in the house, and with all this noise, we can't have church service tonight."

"True, true. I see you bring the little one out with you. Look at the dress! What a pretty dress! Where you get such a pretty dress for her?"

"Not me, but her mother buy it for her in Kingston," Grandy replied, a touch of pride creeping into her voice.

"Turn around, pretty girl, and let me see your dress. What a nice pink colour!"

I spun around so the woman could see the dress fully.

The woman oohed and ahhed, but I had the uncomfortable feeling the woman would have torn the dress off me if she could. A group of churchwomen gathered around Grandy and her church-sister. They were all talking, pretending not to be concerned with what was going on around them, but I knew they were all on the look out for any and everything. By early tomorrow morning they could tell you who was holding onto whom as tight as you pleased, and who was sure to be a new mother this time next year.

I started looking around for my own group of friends, but I saw none of them. The crowd was getting thicker, the music louder and the smell of roasted pig and chicken everywhere. Women were selling gizzadas, coconut cakes, potato pudding and totoes from glass cases. Young children in new clothes were running about the place and a man dressed in a clown outfit was selling pink cotton candy. I was beginning to feel hot and sticky from the full-length slip Grandy insisted I wear under my dress. It was time to make my escape – where were Junie, Sophie and Monique?

"Yes," Grandy was telling her church sister, "I went to see Yvette in the hospital and she doing much better. Coming along real nice. Should be coming home from the hospital any day now."

"Praise the Lord," the woman said, raising a pious hand to the sky. "I pray so much for that child."

"Yes," Grandy nodded. "I said a lot of prayers for her too."

"I hear though," the woman began, clearing her throat to indicate she was going to say something really important, "her father is planning to send her to an aunt in Montego Bay. That's where her mother comes from, you know, worthless good-for-nothing woman. Just up and leave her children like that! How can you just up and leave your own flesh and blood? How can a woman do these things?" She seemed genuinely baffled by what Yvette's mother had done.

"I don't know," Grandy answered. "I still can't figure it out myself. But going to her aunt in Montego Bay might just be the best thing for the girl. Men folks can't raise girl childrens all by themselves. Her father is trying, but that girl needs a woman around."

"Amen to that," another woman observed.

What was being said piqued my interest, because it went directly to something I was trying to figure out. No one in the district knew my father and no one, it seemed, cared to know my father. In the district there were many women raising boys without a father, yet no one questioned this. Why, then, was it so awful what Yvette's mother had done? My father had done the same thing and the only people who ever bad-mouthed him were Grandy or Mama. Yet everywhere people were talking bad about Yvette's mother as if she'd done something far worse than what my own father had done. Why was this? What's more, they spoke of her father in the most glowing terms, as if, in taking care of his children, he was doing something not expected of him and he should be given a trophy for it – and this was the man who they sometimes said "kidnapped" Yvette's mother, old man that he was, young green girl that she had been. None of this made any sense to me. Could, for example, an older woman "kidnap" a younger boy and force him to live with her? Force him to have

60

children with her? What would people say about that? I took a deep breath and counted to ten, trying to decide whether or not to get into Grandy's conversation, for I knew that as far as these women were concerned, children should be seen and not heard, but I decided to go ahead and ask the question that had been bothering me for some time now.

"Grandy," I said softly, pulling on her hand, "how is it that women can raise boy children without a father around, but fathers cannot raise girl children without a woman around?"

At first the women just looked at me in absolute surprise. They looked as if they didn't quite know the creature standing there in front of them. Had I really butted into their big-woman conversation? But I continued with my question, and I thought a look of pure confusion spread over their faces, as if they didn't know how to answer.

Grandy was the first to find her voice. "Well," she said, searching hard to gather her thoughts, "you know children just need their mothers more ..." she turned to her church sisters for help, but the women kept quiet and seemed even more confused by what Grandy said.

"But why?" I persisted, looking back and forth from Grandy to all the other women.

"That's just the way it is!" Grandy said, getting angry because she could not give me a better answer.

Then, as if she realized what I had done – that I had found my way into big people's argument – Grandy exploded. "But look my trouble!" she reached for my ears, but I quickly backed away. "This damn and blasted pickney don't even know when to keep ι. ιr damn and blasted mouth shut!" She made after me again, but I backed away even further.

"Do. 't I tell you one million times, if I tell you one time, when you ι. ιar big people talking, you supposed to stay out of it!" She was breaι ιing fast, a look of weariness on her face. She looked at me as thouζ h I was beyond any kind of help.

The womaι with her now had an evil little smile on her face. I could already ιee her taking every other woman in the church aside, repeating ιhe story over and over again, adding what she wanted to add, sι btracting what she wanted to, of how I'd forced my way into big-people-discussions and was asking big-people-questions about the nature of things I had no business asking about. Everybody would know then what a vagabond of a grand-daughter Grandy had growing up wild in Kingston and that Grandy's daughter was not raising me right.

"I will deal with your case when I get home tonight!" Grandy promised, raising a threatening finger at me. From the look on her face I knew exactly what this meant: She would threaten to pack my bags and send me back to my mother in Kingston on the first bus that passed through the district. This was the threat she often used to keep me in line.

Grandy turned to the woman beside her and tried to excuse my behaviour. "Is not so she grow up you know." She threw me a venomous look. "She grow up with good manners. Honestly, I don't know what get into her today."

"I know, I know," the woman was saying, "is these Kingston children, you know, they are the worse offenders."

Grandy turned slowly to the woman who had gone too far. "Maude, don't get me rass vex out here today! Tell me something, how is Gloria worse off than your two thieving boys?"

The woman kept quiet. Everybody knew her two boys roamed the countryside thieving people's produce and wild stock and selling them in the market at Annatto Bay. It was even said they stole people's clothes off their lines, and once there was a big scandal when a woman saw one of the boy's wearing her husband's shirt and came back with her husband who beat the boy to a pulp.

"And you," Grandy turned back to me, "as soon as we reach home tonight, start packing your clothes so I can send you back to your mother in Kingston!"

If I was really going to be sent home because of this, well, so be it! In fact, as soon as I got home I would start packing! I couldn't wait to get back to Kingston and start All Saints High School. Perhaps there I'd get some answers to my questions! Yes, perhaps in high school I could get some answers to my many many questions!

# CHAPTER 4

The pale-blue and white buildings of All Saint's High School were spread over several acres. The dusty playing field was bordered by thick green shrub, and this my mother and I were crossing. In the centre of the field was a paved volleyball court, and, in the distance, a huge auditorium with blue and red stained-glass windows rose up like a colossus. Classrooms and administrative offices were on either side of the auditorium and a large swimming pool was to its right. The school was so huge. How would I ever find my way round?

In front of the auditorium was a short tree with thick, rough bark and short gnarled branches. It had large sweet-smelling reddish-pink flowers and squat brown fruits. Some of the fruits had fallen to the ground and splattered, giving off a strong unpleasant odour.

"Still here, after all these years," my mother said quietly, looking at the tree.

"What is, Mama?"

"Oh nothing."

I kept a tight hold on my mother's hand. Earlier, after I'd put on my new uniform, I'd stood in front of the mirror looking at myself. The girl in the burgundy tunic and pink blouse looked unfamiliar – me, but not yet me. I was stepping out of an old skin for something I hadn't yet fully grown into. My life was changing, whether for good or bad, I did not know. I suspected that one girl was starting All Saints High School, and at the end, another girl would emerge.

"I wish I had a camera." Mama was looking at me with so many different emotions in her eyes. "I would like to have this picture forever."

She called me over to stand in front of her and fidgeted with my collar, my ribbons, the sleeves of my blouse. When she was satisfied, she finished her own dressing, picked up her handbag and we were ready to leave the house. Just then Rachel came up to the door.

"I just had to come and see you." She looked me up and down. "You looking good, though you need a sweater." I was shivering.

Earlier in the week Rachel had given me some barrettes and clips for my hair and brown socks for school. I had them on now and I could see she was pleased I was wearing them.

"Let we go," Mama said, handing Rachel the house keys. When I came home in the evening I would get them from her.

"Go to school and learn something for you and me," Rachel said, waving to us as we walked towards the front of the yard. She stayed there for a long time, watching me walk, step by step, into my new life.

The closer we got to the auditorium the more my stomach tightened. Would I make friends at All Saints? Would I settle here? Looking around, I could see that some of the other girls knew each other and tight knots of friendship were already forming. I knew absolutely no one.

"You know," Mama patted my hands in hers, "I felt just like you my first day here. Yes, I did. This school has that effect on you, big and imposing as it is. But trust me, you'll get used to it like the rest of us did. If I could get used to it, and I was coming all the way from the back of beyond, from Lluidas Vale Primary School all the way in Portland, you'll certainly manage. All Saints will come to be your school, as it came to be mine. It has a kind of charm that comes over you – even with all its rules and regulations. You'll have a fierce kind of love and dedication for this school. You'll see!"

I looked up at my mother. What must it be like coming back to the school after all those years? Mama never talked about it, about being expelled from All Saints, but over the years Grandy had filled me in. How Mama cried and cried for weeks and weeks on end. How she did everything to expel me from her body. How I stayed put, arriving feet-first five months later. How, when she first saw me, she burst into tears and held me close. Let All Saints High School go. She had a daughter now. Yes, I thought, looking at my mother as her eyes darted all over the place. Yes, it must be quite an experience coming back to All Saints after all those years.

Inside the auditorium the stained-glass windows let in an ethereal blue light. Each frame illustrated an aspect of the life of Jesus. Chairs were carefully arranged in rows and a bright red carpet ran through the centre of the auditorium all the way up to the elevated platform. Nuns directed girls and their parents to seats and the place was filling rapidly. I started looking at the nuns out of the corners of my eyes. I could not help being curious about them. I had heard so many stories about them that I was almost afraid to look at them directly. I had heard they thought themselves holier than everyone else because they were "married" to the Lord. Kept themselves "pure" for the Lord. Rachel was the one who told this to me, snorting in disbelief.

"Can you imagine marrying yourself off to someone way up in the sky, instead of having a flesh and blood man here with you, someone to keep you company at night, someone to..." She remembered who she was talking to and did not finish her statement. Instead, she said, " Well, I guess God will take better care of them than any flesh and blood man, because, God knows, those flesh and blood ones have a way of leaving you when you need them the most!"

I became conscious of my mother's close attention. She was staring at my dark brown socks and new brown shoes, my light pink cotton blouse and thick burgundy tunic. She passed her fingers over my purple heart-shaped school emblem. Then she took my face in her hands, tears welling in her eyes, before she almost pushed me away and we started looking around for seats.

Sister Marie Claire, the principal, ascended the podium and immediately there was a hush. She was a short fat woman who wobbled when she walked. But what an effect this woman had on the audience! Everyone seemed in awe of her.

At that moment one last student and her parents hurried into the auditorium. Both parents looked harassed and embarrassed and the girl untidily dressed. The nuns and teachers seemed to know the harried man and his fat, pleasant-faced wife who smiled and nodded at them. The man was trying to smile but could not. He was struggling with the girl, who had the longest face in the world. The man stopped for a moment, searching for a place for them to sit. The only available seats were behind Mama and me.

"Stop the staring!" Mama shushed me, when she saw that I was looking round at the latecomers. Wild brick-red hair framed the small face of the daughter. Disheveled school uniform. How could her parents let her leave the house looking like that? The night before Mama had combed my hair and tied it down so it would be especially neat in the morning. My uniform had been sent to the cleaners weeks in advance; when it came back the box pleats were like the blade of a knife. How could the girl come to school looking like this?

"*Annie,* why must you *always* be so difficult?" The girl's mother hissed at her, as we stood up for prayer. I looked back and saw her using a hankie to dust her florid face.

"Oh for Christ's sake, Katherine, not now, not here!" the father was saying under his breath.

The girl then fixed me with an irate stare that said I should be minding my own business. Instead of looking away, however, I held the girl's stare for what seemed an eternity, and then she grinned. Mama looked down and elbowed me, but I just kept smiling and smiling. No, this girl could not cow me. Not after the country, not after that girl Yvette who, finally, was out of the hospital.

That evening I raced home to tell Rachel about my first day at All Saints. About Annie, who finagled her way into the same class as I. Annie with whom I sat under the lignum vitae trees after our parents were gone. Annie and I who eyed each other for a very long time before we slowly started talking. Annie who did not want to come to this-stupid-old-school-in-the-first-place, but whose parents were making her. Annie who intentionally an-swered-every-question-wrong-in-order-to-fail-the-common-entrance-exam. Annie whose two older sisters had come to this school but were now in college back in Canada. Oh, she had given our form teacher a hard time this afternoon, had Annie. The Annie who rightfully shouldn't even be in our class! But her father was Chairman of the school board. Had donated a-lot-of-money-to-the-school. Pushing and pulling from the very beginning, our Annie. Even ended up in the chair next to mine. I saw then a girl used to getting her own way. It took me quite some time to see past to something else, another girl curled up tight inside her. We'd been staring at each other hard, and then Annie had looked away, and it seemed for the next couple of years she would keep doing that, keep looking away when I, when anyone, came close to the girl curled up and rocking herself in the far corner.

Rachel was in bed when I came into her room, and I dropped my bag in a chair and immediately started talking.

"Rachel, I have so much to tell you!" I jumped onto her bed.

"And I have all the time in the world to listen, my pet," she said, struggling into a sitting position.

Her voice stopped me; it was brave but weak. Lately she'd been sick and I was beginning to worry about her. Although it was mid-afternoon and had cooled down considerably, Rachel was sweating profusely and her breathing was shallow and laboured. Her maroon-coloured bedspread was soaked with sweat.

"Don't mind me," she said, seeing the look on my face. "Tell me all about it."

"You sure?" I asked, for she really did not look well.

"Sure as I'll ever be. Go ahead and tell me about those other girls and especially about those too-good women in white."

"Well ... they don't all wear white, the nuns, you know."

"Is that so?"

"That is so! Some of the nuns wear blue! Even Mary is painted wearing royal blue!"

She did not laugh at this as I expected. Instead, she looked as if she was in a great deal of pain.

"Rachel, are you sure you're all right?"

"Yes, child, I'm okay. Just the flu. Taking longer for me to get rid of than usual. It leaving me so weak."

"Do you want me to get you anything?"

She considered this for a moment, then nodded her head. "That's not a bad idea at all. I could use some flu medicine. But first you have to take off your school uniform, which is much too big for you!" She was right, the uniform dwarfed me and I felt awkward in it, but Mama insisted before long I would grow into it.

Rachel turned away from me and started fumbling behind her for something under the bed. Finally she gave up and told me to bring her the box and open it for her.

The box I found was emerald green with many different and marvellous animals carved on the outside – lions, tigers, zebras – animals no one ever saw, not even at the zoo here in Jamaica. The box had a silver lock and she passed me the key to open it. This was the first time I saw Rachel's green box, legendary in the yard, even though she always denied its existence. I opened the box gingerly. It was inlaid with red velvet, in stunning contrast to the emerald green on the outside. There were rolls and rolls of money inside the box, both Jamaican money and foreign bills. There was jewellery too, as well as some letters.

Rachel quickly grabbed the box from me once I opened it. She took out some money, as well as our key, and slipped it under the cover with her.

"I hope I don't have to tell you not to tell anyone in the yard about this box." She spoke more seriously to me than I could ever remember.

"No, Rachel, I won't tell anyone."

"Not even your mother, you hear me," Rachel said, in a very threatening voice.

"Not even Mama." I whispered, although this made me uncomfortable. I could keep secrets, my mother often told me, just not from her. In any case, my mother had laughed one day and said, I could never be trusted to keep any secrets, the chatterbox I was. Always telling Grandy her business. Which man came to visit. What she was always doing. But this was one secret I intended to keep. As nice as Rachel could be, I knew there was another side to her, the side that the women in the yard were all a little fearful of, the side that bargained with men over the price of her body. I did not want to get on Rachel's wrong-side.

"That's a good girl," Rachel said, patting my hand. "Now here's the key to your house, go change your clothes and come back for the money to buy the flu medicine."

When I came back from changing my uniform, Rachel was out of bed and the green box was nowhere to be seen. I took the money from her and left for the shop. At the front of the yard, however, I ran into a barrage of policemen with raised submachine guns. They were making a raid, searching for illegal substances such as marijuana, or for weapons. For all the years I'd lived in the yard, I'd never gotten used to the sight of loaded guns; they left me speechless and in shivers. I stood for a while, wondering what to do, almost wetting myself, I was so frightened. They were lining up the men and older boys against the wall, barking orders at them and searching them.

Soon they would start going through the rooms, pulling people out and tearing the place apart, on the hunt for anything illegal. People had to produce receipts for everything they owned, no matter how old it was. Often receipts had been lost or never existed in the first place – people given old hand-me-down furniture, or gifts of appliances from friends or family abroad. They had to bargain with the police to leave their things alone. Otherwise the police could seize whatever they wanted, and it would never be seen again. The people in the yard always tried to get advance warning of a raid so they could hide their valuables.

I turned back into the yard and ran quickly to Rachel's room. "What is it?" she asked, alarmed to see me breathless. "Police." I did not need to say another word.

Rachel sprang into action, taking off her gold bangles and her large gold butterfly earrings. She swept her hand under the bed, pulled out the green box and dumped all her jewellery inside it. She moved back the mat under her chair, pressed hard on the floor with her foot and two boards came loose. She dropped the green box into the hole, replaced the floorboards, the mat, and finally the chair.

I stood there, astonished.

Rachel moved so fast, it seemed she'd been through the routine many times before. She had just eased herself back into bed when the police arrived.

"Open up, open up!" they banged on the door which was already open.

Rachel shuffled out of bed, holding the top of her nightgown together so as not to expose her breasts.

"Raaaachel!" The head officer was laughing. "Fancy finding you home this evening. Business not good down at the wharf?"

Rachel looked at him as if she didn't understand what he was saying.

He used his gun to push the door all the way open and I backed up against the wall, expecting the worst.

"What's this about, officer?" Rachel was trying her best to put on her usual gruff voice, but it wasn't working.

"What happened to Rachel today? Tired from working all night?" The officer looked back at the other constables, who all started laughing.

"Look, officer, I'm not feeling well; you mind telling me what this is about."

"We searching, Rachel. A store on Slipe Road was broken into early this morning and we looking for stolen goods."

"Nothing stolen in here," Rachel replied, her face darkening in anger.

"Well, let's just take a quick look around."

"You're welcome!" She moved away from the door. She knew what they were about to do, but was powerless to stop them.

Several policemen came into the room and started ploughing through Rachel's belongings. They overturned the mattress, pulled her clothes out of the closet and emptied out her chest-of-drawers. They went through the dishes on the table, letting some of them slip through their fingers and break on the ground; they dipped their fingers into the stew on the stove; overturned the water in the basin, and turned over bags of rice, sugar, salt and red kidney beans in the water. They parcelled out Rachel's oranges, bananas and june-plums and started eating them right there before her.

"Where is it?" the officer finally demanded.

"Where is what?" Rachel looked very puzzled.

"The money box. We know you have a money box in here."

"I don't know where you get that from."

"Come now, Rachel, we not stupid. We know the business you're into. Where all the gold bangles and earrings?"

Rachel did not answer.

"We can make this easy or we can make this hard."

It was like something I had seen on television taking place in some far-off country, only then the faces were much paler. The police continued their search, scattering the plastic flowers, tearing down the curtains, their heavy boots making a mockery of Rachel's well-polished floor. My heart almost leapt out of my chest when they neared the chair.

"Rachel, come on, you mean to tell me a woman in your profession don't have a money box? No green box in here?"

"Officer, I don't know what you're talking about. I thought you were looking for stolen goods."

"That too."

"Well, as you can see, no stolen goods in here. No ganja in here. No guns in here. No green money box in here."

The officer eyed her up and down disdainfully, before giving the order for the men to withdraw. "All right, you get away this time, but don't think you always going get away. I watching you. I know about the money box and I intend to find it."

Rachel collapsed on the mattress from the effort it had taken her to be brave. My legs were trembling so badly I thought they would buckle under me. The house was a royal mess and would need a lot of cleaning up.

"Gloria, go get the medicine for me. I *really* need it now."

As I made my way through the yard I saw the police going into other rooms – all except my mother's, which was locked tight. They knew my mother as a decent, hard-working woman and we were almost always left alone. I was afraid to so much as look at them and if they stopped me and asked me where I was going, no words would come out of my mouth. Thank goodness Jesus was out with one of his women, for he always suffered the most from the police.

I hurried out into the street where I let out a sigh of relief. The news of the raid had moved quickly through the neighbourhood and there was no one in sight. The boys who usually sat idle on the sidewalks were gone. The drug dealers with their money, jewellery and expensive rental cars were gone. Everyone was deep in hiding.

## CHAPTER 5

Before long Annie and I were inseparable. We sat beside each other in class, went to lunch together, sat together in laboratory classes, during mass, and somehow always ended up on the same teams during games. We started exploring the school, going behind the science laboratories, where we found a thick patch of sugar cane that had obviously been growing there for years, and which everyone had forgotten about. For days Annie and I ate so many pieces of sugar cane our jaws ached. On another expedition we found, hidden behind the fourth form classrooms, a large naseberry tree with many ripe fruit. Naseberries were my favourite fruits and Annie loved them too. She said it was this fruit that helped her adjust when she first came from Canada to live in Jamaica. Its taste had sucked her in, and after her first naseberry she'd started to view the island differently. Now, even though she still yearned for all the people she was close to in Canada, she had come to see Jamaica as her home and had developed a fierce love for the island.

When we found the naseberry tree, at first we just stood under it, looking up, hoping some ripe naseberries would fall. The trouble was that when they did fall, they would break open, their sweet brown insides splattering all over the ground. Every day when we went there, naseberries lay plastering the ground. It seemed criminal that they should be going to waste.

"I know what we can do," Annie said one day, in what I feared was a dangerous voice.

"And what is that?" I was beginning to understand she was a soul who would do anything, say anything. Time and time again she reminded me of another reckless soul I knew in the country.

"I will climb the tree."

Already my mind was doing cartwheels over what would happen if we were caught. Climbing trees was something we were not supposed to do, especially here at All Saints High School. It was unlady-like, and doing unlady-like things could get us in serious trouble. Even my grandmother said so. This was not to say I couldn't wrap my legs around a tree trunk and shimmy up a tree as well as anyone – but it was an unlady-like thing to do.

"Think of all the fruits in the tree," Annie was saying, knowing this would silence my doubts. Naseberries had that kind of hold over me: their insides the colour of raw honey; the sweetness dissolving in my mouth. Already I could taste them. I looked up at the ripe fruits. It seemed a shame they should go to all the ants and birds around.

"No one will see us." The tree *was* set away from the school and, unless someone else knew about it, nobody would come looking.

Before I could stop her, Annie was out of her shoes and socks, had shinned up the tree trunk, moved skillfully from branch to branch, where she picked and threw down ripe naseberries to me. Oh, what a feast we had that day and for weeks after! Then it was the Julie mango trees at the back of the school, behind the art and music buildings, where we picked the mangoes before they were fully ripe, when they were "turn", and ate them covered with salt and pepper.

Still we kept doing our schoolwork, Annie and I, and pretty soon we had gained a reputation as the two brightest girls in our entire form. All our teachers remarked on this, that no matter all the things we got up to, we always managed to get the highest grades in all the exams. Annie and I were two planets that revolved around each other. Not even my mother or grandmother entered that universe and, truthfully, neither seemed to matter as much to me as Annie any more. If anyone had asked me to describe Annie, the first word that would have come out of my mouth was "perfect". She was wise above everyone else, led the way in personality, could do no wrong. Any contrary opinion was met with disdain on both our parts, for I knew she felt the same way about me. Nobody at All Saints knew what to make of our friendship, since we came from such different worlds. Me, the daughter of a hard-working single mother; chauffeur-driven Annie who lived with both parents in the hills. But after a few puzzled stares, people just left us alone.

Annie loved complaining about her parents, especially her father. "They throw these horrible dinner parties. For horrible people from abroad. People who want to tell us how things should be done here in Jamaica. And my father always agrees with them. He believes everything is just hopeless. Says America should come and take over Jamaica. Can you beat that?"

It was her father's lack of tolerance for anything Jamaican that most infuriated her. Her mother seemed to like Jamaica well enough, which was odd because she was the one who was not Jamaican, but came from Canada. Her parents had met while her father was a scholarship student at the L'Université de Laval in Canada. They'd married in Canada, had their children there, then moved to Jamaica a few years ago.

"Why did your father want to come back to Jamaica in the first place?" I asked Annie one day.

"What do you think? To fix things. To run things. Oh, he gave the usual story about missing his country and wanting to do good, blah, blah, blah. But I always knew what his real motives were, and that's why we always have these American foundation people parading through our house. The last one who came, she was just the most horrible." Annie rolled her eyes up to the sky. "This Jane woman from New York! Telling the Director of the National Gallery that he should let her to take our ancient Taino sculptures back with her to New York! They would be better placed at some museum in America! When the director balked at her request, she was in our house planning how to get the man fired!" I vaguely remembered hearing something about the sculptures on the news a few months back, about a farmer who had found them, hidden them for years, before he finally turned them over to the National Gallery; some anthropologists from abroad had found out about them and were trying to steal them from him.

"The nerve of that woman, to say nothing of my own father!"

Annie was such a restless spirit. Caught up in one cause or another. Keeping what she called "A scrap book of atrocities." It

74

was as if she saw every injustice in the world and was trying to find answers to truly difficult problems. In this respect she was very different from most of the other girls like her at All Saints who were completely relaxed in their privilege, happy to let their family name and skin colour give them a free ride through Jamaican society. But not Annie. In class she was a thorn in our teachers' sides. Such terrible confrontations. "If only they'd just give us a straight answer!" Annie would say in frustration when one of our teachers chastised her about her incessant questions, "instead of this back-and-belly beating-around-the-bush business they go in for!"

One day our form teacher, Mrs. Clarke, dragged a life-sized doll into the classroom. The doll opened up and Mrs. Clarke showed us the various parts of our bodies. Slender fallopian tubes, oval-shaped ovaries, the soft cushion of blood and tissue which dissolved in menstruation. She even had a picture showing us strong tadpoles swimming through the vagina to join with an egg, resulting in pregnancy. How those tadpoles got there in the first place was never discussed. Pregnancy – having sex – was to be avoided at all costs. It was the mantra chanted into us daily; the mantra that we chanted to ourselves.

"What happens if you get pregnant?" Mrs. Clarke would ask.

"We will have to leave All Saints High School."

"And what will happen if you have to leave All Saints before time?"

"We will not get into another school as good!"

"And what will that result in?"

"The end of our education."

Because of guidance class, however, some things began to make sense to me: the strange new smell I had developed over the past few weeks. No matter how I washed and washed myself in the mornings, the smell was there by mid-afternoon. Mama must have noticed the smell too because she came home one day and handed me, without explanation, my very own bottle of deodorant. It was like the tadpoles again. I wished Mama would talk to me, explain what was going on, but she never did. Somehow I would get to know everything that I was supposed to know. Or All Saints would fill in all the gaps. It was all so bewildering.

Dark unruly tufts of hair started appearing under my arms, and almost all of my blouses became tight across my chest. My arms and legs now stuck out of everything I owned. Mama complained she would have to be a millionaire to keep up with how quickly I was growing. It was all fascinating if a little unnerving. I felt as though I was becoming a new animal, but one I did not fully recognize. It was as if I was looking at myself through running water: there was a semblance of my old self, but it was distorted and fragmented and was constantly changing.

Some days I agreed with everything Mama said and wanted nothing more than to climb into her lap and nestle close to her, my head on her bosom. Then I could be her little girl again, the one who adored her and the one who she adored, the little girl dressed up to match her mother. Mama had photos she'd taken of us at various stages of our lives. Some were taken in the park in downtown Kingston with red and yellow canna lily flowers all around us. Others were taken in photographers' studios. There was one photo when I was probably no more than a year old. I am standing on a wicker chair which fans out behind me like the feathers of a peacock. I am wearing a short white dress, white bloomers underneath, white ribbons in my hair. On my feet are black patent leather shoes, and in my hand, a black patent leather handbag. Two gold bangles on my wrists. I look a little frightened, as if I'm about to cry, as if I'm looking for my mother. Sometimes I looked and looked at this photograph, finding it hard to believe I was ever that little girl – no, baby – so many years before. Mama found this hard to believe too, and there were times when she took the picture up, looked at me, then back at the picture, before shaking her head in disbelief. I suspected a part of her wanted that child back. That little girl back. The mutual adoration.

Other days I could not get far enough away from Mama. Anger seemed to shadow all our interactions. For reasons I could not explain, *no* was the word I used most often with her. Before she could finish asking me a question, my answer was "no".

"Stop that!" she shouted at me one day. "There are other words in the English language than that one word. Everything 'no this; no that'. Don't use that word with me ever again!"

I had the feeling sometimes that I was in free fall.

The only times I felt comfortable, which was to say, the only times I felt at peace with myself and my body, were the times I was with Annie, because we both seemed to be in a place that was dark one minute, then brightly lit the next. With Annie, I did not have to do any explaining.

In the yard, Nilda was rapidly changing too, slowly but surely becoming a different person. I rarely had the time to stop and talk to her because of my own hectic schedule, though she always smiled and waved at me, as I smiled and waved to her. But she seemed always vaguely unhappy, even more distant of late, as if she was forever contemplating something. I knew she had so much more to do now that her mother was working as a helper in one of the houses in the hills. Her mother had to get to work very early in the morning and came back home late at night. Most of the responsibility for the house and for the four younger children fell on Nilda's shoulders and she was often harried and busy. Occasionally, however, Nilda would come over to my verandah and we would sit and talk, but she made sure we never talked about her life. I kept promising myself that one day we would sit down and have a proper talk, get her to tell me about whatever it was she always seemed to be thinking about.

One evening as I approached the front of the yard, I noticed a new white car. It stood out against the cracked and crumbling pavements and the walls covered with political slogans. A group of men were gathered around the car and one man in particular stood out. While all the other men were wearing old merinos and cut-off pants, one, obviously the owner of the car, was dressed all in white to match. He had on a white fur hat, a white silk shirt and several gold chains. On his fingers were huge gold rings. Leaning against the car he surveyed the area coolly. A drug dealer. One just back from New York. No doubt filling the ears of the men around him with the wonders of America. Jesus was there, leaning very close to him, holding onto his every word.

I had to admit that I, too, was curious about this place called America. It seemed to have quite an effect on people. No matter how rundown someone was in Jamaica, it seemed a trip to America, or Canada, could turn their fortunes around tremendously. Before long they could buy houses in some of the best neighbourhoods, and give their children the things they always wanted them to have. Most people I knew, including my mother, prayed for a visa to go to America. In America, she could work a few months as a housekeeper or a baby-sitter, as she'd heard many Jamaican women did, then she'd come back home with the oh-so-valuable Yankee dollars. Or, she could use the money she earned in America to buy things she would bring back to sell at exorbitant prices here in Jamaica. My mother had tried several times to get a visa, and every time was unsuccessful. The Americans kept giving her the same reason every time they denied her – she did not have enough "ties" to keep her in Jamaica, and there was no guarantee she would come back to the island if they gave her a visa.

"But I have my daughter here!" Mama pointed to me dressed up beside her in my school uniform the last time we went to the American embassy; but of no use.

"You could easily leave your daughter with someone and take off," the woman behind the glass with the crisp American accent told her. "You people do this kind of thing all the time." She paused for a moment when she saw the disappointment on my mother's face.

"Look," she said, softening, "come back when you have a better job. A home. Some investments. Come back when you have something significant that can tie you to Jamaica. Then we will gladly give you a visa."

The same thing happened a couple of days later at the Canadian embassy.

And a few weeks later at the British High Commission.

After that Mama said she would never again try to get visa to leave Jamaica. For better or worse, she was going to stick to the island; we'd have to make it here. She could not be bothered with these English, American and Canadian people and their oh-so-precious-visas.

The man in white looked over at me as I was turning into the yard. He seemed vaguely familiar, but I couldn't quite place him. He, on the other hand, seemed to know exactly who I was, and, indeed, seemed to have been waiting for me. He turned and asked

Jesus something and Jesus nodded. The man then left the group and sauntered over.

I hurried in to try to avoid him.

"You don't need to be afraid," he said, in a deep voice with a slight American accent. He was smooth and dark. His smell was different; the air around him was different; even the dark of his skin was different. It was easy to tell that he came from abroad. "You don't remember me, Gloria? Little Gloria, get so big now. Almost grow out of my sight. You don't remember me?"

I kept looking hard at him, trying to place him, but I could not.

"Well, when your mother come home tonight tell her Zekie came by to see her. Remember the name now: Zekie."

Jesus walked over to us. "Yes, you know Zekie! Zekie used to live in the yard with us." He pointed into the yard, as if this would help me remember.

I shook my head indicating that I did not remember the man, and went inside. There was something about this man I did not like. There was the way he smiled when he spoke about my mother, a smile that seemed to say he knew her very well; knew her in a way that immediately made me uncomfortable. I would ask Rachel who this man was as soon as I got into her room.

Again I found Rachel in bed, still struggling to get over the flu. A film of dust covered the room and the fruits in the bowl had all shrivelled up, something that never usually happened. There was water on the floor, as if she'd tried to get some from the pail, but had spilled it. "I'm so weak, Gloria," she said as I walked into the room.

Immediately I got busy. I opened the window to let fresh air into the room, gathered up the dirty dishes and took them outside to the standpipe and washed them. I helped Rachel into a chair, and changed the sheet on her bed. I mopped up the water, swept the floor and threw out all the rotting fruit. I looked around for something for her to eat, because it did not look as if she'd eaten all morning.

"Ah Gloria child, what would I do without you?"

She fumbled around with the green box, trying to open it, before she finally gave up and handed it to me. "Take your key out, and I want to give you a little something for your help."

"Oh no," I said, backing away from her, finding it hard to

believe she felt she should pay me for helping her. "You don't have to give me any money for this." I must have said this with a lot of hurt, because she looked away shamefaced. "But you really should go to the hospital again."

"Lord, I been to that hospital so many times already! They don't how to cure a little flu!"

"Well, you need to go to a private doctor! Everyone knows a private doctor is better than the doctors at the public hospitals!"

"Next week, I mean it, Gloria, I going to see Dr. David next week in Cross Roads."

"And I'll go with you," I said, promising myself that even if I had to sneak out of school, I'd go with her.

Just as I was about to go I remembered the stranger. "Rachel, a man outside, a foreigner, says I should say hello to my mother for him. Says his name is Zekie."

"His name again?" Rachel leaned closer, a look of surprise on her face.

"Zekie," I replied, getting annoyed with the look on her face.

She started smiling slowly, and said, more to herself than to me, *The little devil!* And he didn't even come to say hello to me. Although I wouldn't want anyone seeing me in this condition ... *The little devil!*"

"Who *is* he?" I asked impatiently.

"You don't remember Zekie? He used to live in this yard with us, but left for America a few years ago. Lord, he had it bad for your mother. Bad, bad, bad for your mother. Used to bother-bother her all the time, that Zekie. Your mother wouldn't give him the time of day. He was always telling her he was going go to America, make a lot of money and come back to Jamaica and marry her. *The little devil!*" She shook her head in disbelief.

From the look on her face I could tell I wouldn't get any more information out of Rachel. I took up my school things and left. I didn't like what was going on one bit. This Zekie person looked like he was about to become a problem. A major problem.

Mama was home for hours before I finally delivered the message. I only delivered it because I didn't want someone else to tell her before I did. I was quite surprised someone hadn't already stopped her on the street and told her about Zekie.

"Mama, this man, says his name is Zekie, said to tell you hello."
I said this as casually as I could, hoping to get an equally casual
response. We had just finished dinner and were relaxing in front
of the television.

"Tell me again what you just said?" Mama got up and turned
off the television, so she could better hear me. "Who you said gave
you that message?"

"Zekie," I repeated. She actually seemed to glow when she
heard the man's name.

"When did he give you this message?" She was touching her
hair and patting down her clothes, as if to make sure she was
presentable. She started moving around the house touching
things. She did this when she was either very excited about
something, or very unsure about what was going on. "Zekie?" she
asked again. "Did I hear you correctly, Gloria? Did you say this
man's name was Zekie?"

I reluctantly nodded my head.

"Tell me exactly what he said. Did he say he was coming back
tonight?"

I was no longer a person in the room, just a source of much-
needed information.

"Did he say if he was coming back tonight?" She was now busy
putting things in order around the house, touching anything she
could get her hands on, fixing her hair and clothes, looking at
herself in the mirror.

"No, he did not say that he was coming back tonight."

"Tell me again what he said!" A kind of disbelieving laughter
bubbled up in her throat.

"I was coming home from school..."

"No, not that part. What exactly did he say?"

A bitter taste started rising in my mouth as I looked at my
mother who had a soft dreamy look in her eyes and a smile
softening the corners of her mouth. A foolish schoolgirl look. A
look I immediately hated. Zekie was about to become someone
very important in her life; and, consequently, someone very
important in both our lives. No, I did not like what was going on
at-all, at-all!

# CHAPTER 6

Mama did not go to work the next morning, but stayed home anxiously waiting for Zekie to come and visit her. The look of expectation and excitement on her face was too much for me, and I stormed out, slamming the door behind me. If this had registered on Mama, as it most certainly would usually have done, she would have hauled me back into the house by my collar as if I was a fowl whose neck she was about to wring, but she was evidently so absorbed in the thought of seeing Zekie.

At school my feelings must have been written all over my face because Annie kept asking me what the problem was.

"Oh nothing," I answered offhandedly. Who was this person who seemed to mean so much to my mother? How long would he be staying in Jamaica? I couldn't wait for him to go back to America.

Annie kept looking at me. She knew something at home was bothering me, but I was not talking.

"Rachel?" she asked, because I sometimes spoke to her about the people in the yard. She knew all about Nilda, Denise, Rachel and some of the others.

"No," I answered miserably, "this has nothing to do with Rachel." I knew that I was being irrational in my anger, knew that if Mama had wanted to, she could have accused me of tossing her aside for Annie, could have said that we no longer cleaned the house together on Saturday mornings as we used to, that I no longer went with her to the market, watching as she chose which bunch of escallion, or what piece of yellow, white or negro yam to buy. She could have pointed out that I no longer went with her to the haberdashery on Harbour Street and watched as she ached and ached over which piece of cloth to buy for a dress, which buttons to put on that dress, and what was the right thread to use to make a blouse, or skirts for the pair of us. Now I couldn't conceal my boredom when she started fingering pieces of lace to put around a blouse, turning the lace this way then that in the light, holding it against the material she was thinking of edging, holding the lace first against my skin, then her own, to see how it would look on us. All of this had abruptly ended when I started going to All Saints High School.

Of course, there'd been a stream of "friends" over the years, men who'd flitted in and out of my mother's life, men who were drawn to her as a butterfly to a flower, or a moth to the strong blaze of a fire. The difference was that I'd never seen her act quite like this over any man, other than my father, and that was a long time ago. My mother was aloof with the men in her life. No matter what they did – chocolates, postcards, flowers and ice creams – my mother was polite, even cordial, but it did not go any further than that. They were all just her "friends". Nothing more. But from the look on her face, this Zekie person was clearly different.

"Well how about coming to spend the weekend at my house – *this* weekend?" Annie asked, looking hard at me, daring me to say no. This was not the first time she'd asked me over and it would not be the last time I would have to decline. Every time I begged Mama to let me go, she always refused, saying she did not like the idea of me sleeping at other people's houses; bad things happened to little girls this way.

"Perhaps," Rachel suggested when I told her about this, "she just trying to spare you the embarrassment of Annie wanting the offer returned. How would you feel about having Annie over to your house?"

I did not answer. A curious thing had started happening to me since attending All Saints High School. Whereas before I felt no shame about the place where I lived, took it as a fact of my life like I took the dark brown colour of my skin, since attending All Saints, I had begun to feel shame about where I lived, and had gone to great pains to hide this from the other girls at school. I never hid where I lived from Annie, who made me know that

83

even if I lived in a pit at the bottom of the earth, it would not matter. She would still be my friend.

"Course," Rachel had continued, "if she your friend for true, it don't matter where you live. A true friend understand this isn't something you control."

Yes, I silently agreed, it shouldn't matter where I lived, but at a place like All Saints it did matter and many of the girls would not let you forget it. That same day I was admiring a flower one of Rachel's suitors had sent her: a purple and white orchid propped up against a slender stick in a clay flowerpot. It was the first time I'd seen such a delicate flower and gently fingered its soft green leaves and fragile purple and white petals. Among the many artificial flowers in her room, the single orchid looked out of place, almost as if it was the false flower and all the plastic flowers were real. I felt like that single displaced flower.

"No," I said to Annie, "I can't come to your house this weekend." It would be useless to bother asking my mother.

Mama was in a pair of shorts with her hair pulled back when I walked into the house. She had a girlish look on her face and was laughing. Zekie was with her and it seemed she'd been laughing all day.

"Gloria! You're home early." She looked down at her wrist for the watch that was always there, but was not there today.

"Gloria," she smiled and turned back to the man in the room, "remember Zekie?"

"No, I do not remember Zekie."

Still looking at Zekie and without once looking at me, Mama continued, "Gloria, Zekie and I go back a long way. A long-long way. We are good friends. Real *good* friends." She had a glow and a stupid look on her face. The eyes I thought were mine and only mine were now focused on another. I put my school bag down and hoped Zekie would soon go back to America.

Almost over night my mother became a new person. She hurried home after work to cook some elaborate meal for Zekie. Rice and peas, which was a Sunday dinner, became a daily ritual. As she grated and carefully squeezed the creamy white milk out of the coconut, she smiled, though it was something she ordinarily hated to do. She hummed as she chopped, bundled and added little sacks of garlic, escallion, and thyme to the dish. Since Zekie liked fish she haunted the fish markets downtown during her lunch break to find the biggest and fattest parrot and snapper fishes to cook for him. She cooked the fish with onions, plummy red tomatoes and okroes, just the way he liked it.

When Zekie was there in the evenings, and it seemed he was at our home every evening, she became impatient with me, complaining that I was lingering over my dinner or my homework, which was not a lie for I was looking to see just how long this charade would go on. Despite my protests she hurried me off to bed just as dusk walked with its big square toes across the sky.

If she saw from my face I was upset, she either ignored me or got angry with me, saying that just because I was in high school I shouldn't get it into my head I was a woman now. There was only one woman in the house, and that was she. Zekie was all she seemed to care about, and she spent hours with him on the verandah in the evenings, her laughter carrying to me in the bedroom, where I was always searching for something to plug my ears with. I knew it wouldn't be long before I woke up one morning and found him living in the house with us, because he did not seem to be in any hurry to get back to America.

We barely spoke to each other, Zekie and I. He gave me bottles of expensive perfumes, a bag, shoes, slippers, all manner of things he'd brought back with him from America. Every time he gave me something, he would wait around to see if the gift brought us closer. It never did. I let him know, in no uncertain terms, that I did not like him and, if I had my way, I would get him out of my mother's life. Of course, I was never foolish enough to *say* this to his face, and would behave myself tolerably enough when my mother was around, but when she was not there, I would put on quite a show. Either I would pretend he wasn't there, or I would go out of my way to make him angry. If he asked me a question, for example, about where to find something in the house, I would refuse to answer. When he went through the door, I made a show of locking it with the dead bolt, as loudly as I could, so he would get the message.

For a while he tried talking to me, but when, after many attempts, he saw I had no intention of speaking to him, he stopped. I became a master of deception, smiling at him when my mother was around, so that when he finally complained about me, she could not believe what he was saying. Yes, she knew I had my moments, I heard her telling him one night, but really I was not a vindictive child. When he could not take it any more, he accosted me in the house.

"Gloria, what is it? Why are you carrying on like this? ... Is it because of your father?"

My father? What a joke! I hadn't seen the man in years, and really did not give much thought to him. My father? I laughed and walked away, leaving Zekie standing there. All I wanted to know was when he was going back to America. He was beginning to act as though he had come home for good. It was obvious he had a lot of money. He changed cars as often as he changed his clothes, and, every evening, some impoverished youth would come to our house asking his help. It was no secret how he had made his money, although my mother kept pretending he was a business-man come home to the island from America. He'd grown tired of the cold and lonely winters in New York and had moved back to be in the sun and to open his own business. I just kept looking at her the first time she told me that story. Everyone knew the truth was different, though no-one seemed to disapprove. What a difference going to America could make in someone's life every-one kept saying! If only *they* could get a visa to go to America!

Jesus, in particular, was very vocal about what he would do – all the cars he would buy. The clothes. The houses. The jewel-lery. He trailed behind Zekie everywhere, listening closely to everything Zekie had to say about America. He often had a faraway look on his face, as if trying to picture himself there.

Nadia had not forgiven Jesus for the last outside child he fathered, and they still avoided each other about their house and in the yard. Sometimes she quarrelled with him, saying that instead of running around behind Zekie all the time like some lap dog, couldn't he give Nilda a hand with the chores? Didn't he see all the work his daughter had to do?

Jesus yawned but never replied.

One evening I came home early and found Mama and Zekie in a tight embrace. Zekie pulled away quickly from Mama when I walked in, but not before I saw that his hands had been around her waist and he had been kissing her on the nape of her neck. She was swaying against him and had that dreamy faraway look on her face I now thoroughly detested. When she saw me standing there looking at her, her cheeks darkened in embarrassment.

"You don't have sense enough to know you're supposed to knock on a door before entering? Where all your manners gone? What happen?" she walked over to me. "You don't have a tongue in your mouth to answer? You cannot talk?"

I was ashamed of my mother. Ashamed that she was behaving no better than one of the young girls about the yard – even worse, it seemed to me, because she was my mother and I expected more from her. I looked at her in disgust, and she seemed totally taken aback by the intensity of my stare.

At that moment something changed between us. From that moment on I was no longer the child she could give orders to and who would willingly obey her. Something had entered our relationship and entered it with a force. It came and stood right between us and brought all its anger, hurt, disappointment and resentment. A few weeks before there was a TV programme about a man who charmed and handled snakes in far-away Morocco. It seemed that this was what was going on between my mother and me. We each had our long black snakes, and we each knew how to handle them expertly. We both decided to pull our snakes back and move out of each other's way.

I stood there for a moment just staring at her, before I dropped my bag on the floor and left the house for Rachel's room. I had to get out of my mother's presence, because I felt I was about to burst into tears. From the bits and pieces I heard about the yard and from the snippets of information Rachel threw my way, I had come to understand Zekie's place in my mother's life. Zekie was one of the barefooted boys about the yard when my mother and I first moved there. From the minute she moved into the yard Zekie developed an intense liking for Mama and would do just about anything to please her.

"He was a mess about your mother, child." Rachel told me

later that evening, after I'd had a good cry and calmed down a bit. "I remember how that boy say to me, 'Rachel,' he was watching your mother catch some water at the standpipe, 'introduce me to your friend.'

"I look at Zekie like he crazy, and say to him, 'What business my friend could have with you? What can you possibly do for my friend?' Those days your mother hardly spoke to anyone in the yard."

"'You never know,' Zekie tell me. 'One day I going get she, whether you believe it or not. One day Rosalie going be my wife!'

"'Keep dreaming,' I tell him. But one thing I always like about Zekie was he have the best humour in the world. Start whistling at your mother on the street and when that don't work he go to Cross Roads and wait on her until she coming home from work, then he would walk her home in the evenings. If she have to go to market, he there to carry her bags. It look like everywhere your mother turn, there was Zekie."

"At first she never pay him much attention, after the problems with your father she was a bit disgusted with mens. But after a while she start getting to like Zekie. Not much, just a little bit. Then his dream came true and he left for America. That was years ago, my dear. You just a little girl then. Funny to see this boy who use to bounce from pillow to post in this yard turn out to be somebody so important."

I shrugged my shoulders. I just wished he would go back to America. Rachel kept watching me.

"Gloria," Rachel asked, softening, "what bothering you? Why you don't like Zekie?"

Truthfully, I did not know why I didn't like him. I would even have agreed that it had nothing to do with how he was, but more with how my mother was acting. Since he'd come into her life, she'd been able to buy many of the things she'd wanted for the house. There were new curtains blowing at the windows, pots and pans in the kitchen, a new television set, a blender, a juicer, all manner of things she'd wanted to have for the longest time, but just could not afford.

"What is it?" Rachel continued. "Gloria, did Zekie do *anything* to you?"

Rachel was always alert to such things, because, she told me once, *something-like-that* had happened to her when she was nine and she'd promised herself she would try to protect as many children as she could from the same thing happening.

"No, no," I said, quickly. Much as I disliked Zekie, I did not want to spread vicious rumours about him.

Rachel looked relieved. "And school?"

"Well that is a whole other story!"

"Problems at school?" she asked again, after I'd been quiet for a couple of minutes.

"No, no problems at school."

"You sure now?"

"Yes, I'm sure."

"That's what I want to hear. And how is your Grandy doing these days anyway? We haven't seen her around these parts in quite a while."

We hadn't seen Grandy much recently because of her arthritis, which was steadily getting worse. She could not get around as much as before, and this was really beginning to bother her, because she was a woman used to moving around when she had a mind to. But she kept sending letters to Mama and me – keeping us abreast of all the latest developments in Lluidas Vale.

"Grandy is fine. She even asked about you the other day."

"What she ask about?" Rachel said laughing. "Whether I in my grave yet?"

It was the wrong joke. Even though she was playing her sickness down, I knew she worried about it. What was this sickness that had taken hold of her, this sickness with the flu-like symptoms that had found its way inside her and was refusing to let go? Rumour had it that some of Rachel's other "friends" from the wharf were getting sick with the same symptoms. Some of them so sick they could not work. One woman had actually died. I knew Rachel was worrying if she had the dreaded new disease everyone was whispering about; the one without a cure.

"Whether you believe it or not," I said, trying to lighten things up, "Grandy did ask about you in her last letter. She said: how is *your friend* doing."

"Well *that* I can believe." Rachel gave a nervous little laugh.

We had been talking for hours. It was pitch-black outside. Mama hated it when I stayed this late with Rachel and I was surprised she hadn't come to get me already. No doubt laughing and laughing at something Zekie had said.

"I guess I should be going now," I said, getting up to leave.

"I guess you should. And don't fuss with your mother so much."

"But she's the one who's always making trouble with me!"

"Perhaps, but that never bother you before."

"It did, but I couldn't say anything to her before. I'm not exactly a baby any more you know."

"I have noticed." Rachel looked me up and down nodding. "You're growing up fast. Very fast. But remember, Gloria, the world is large, and there's still so much you don't know. Try and have patience with your mother."

"I'll try," I promised, reaching over and giving Rachel a hug. "I'll see you tomorrow."

"I'll be here," she said. "You know where to find me."

Outside it was very dark and there was no moon in the sky. It was on nights such as this that I remembered a story Uncle Silas told me.

"Back in slavery days," he said, "there was a pair of slave lovers who were doomed from the start. They loved each other very much and every chance they got would meet on a high bluff on the plantation where the girl lived. They met on moonless nights when it was very dark, because they couldn't risk the light of the moon. Now, this girl, she was very dark and something else to look at. The master of the plantation wanted her for himself. But no matter what he did, the master could never win the young slave girl's favours. This puzzled him, because even though he could take the girl against her will, he wanted her to submit to him willingly. He started asking around and learnt the girl's heart belonged to another man. A younger man, a slave called John from a neighbouring plantation. He was furious. How could the girl, herself a slave, choose a slave over him? He arranged to have the girl's lover sold. The day before the sale was to take place, he followed the lovers up to the bluff where they were meeting for the last time. When the couple saw the master coming, they held hands and jumped over the bluff. Since that day the place has been called Lovers Leap. They did not die, however," Uncle Silas had said, "for the moon, who had been hiding all this time, suddenly came out from behind the clouds and stretched out her long white arms and caught the lovers and carried them with her far up in the sky. So, on moonless nights, the moon is still there, hiding, waiting on her chance to show herself. Waiting on her chance to lead someone home."

This story had comforted me on many a moonless night.

As I felt my way from Rachel's room, savouring the good feelings I always had when I visited her, a hand reached out and touched me.

"Don't scream!" Even as a whisper I recognized Nilda's voice.

"Nilda, don't you ever do anything stupid like that again!" I said fiercely, fighting to catch my breath. The girl could've given me a heart attack.

"I'm sorry, Gloria, but I've been waiting on you for a long time. I need to talk to you. I need to talk to somebody."

There was a desperation in her voice I'd never heard before. "Nilda, what is it?" I asked, quickly forgetting my anger.

"Not here, let's find somewhere private to talk." She looked around the yard.

"Under the tamarind tree?" My eyes were adjusting to the darkness and I could see there was no one there. "We have to be careful, though. We both know Miss Christie always have her ears up against the wall, listening for other people's business."

"Let me just get my bag." Nilda said, reaching behind her.

"What bag?" I asked, alarmed.

"The one I'm taking with me. I've had enough. I'm leaving."

"Leaving? Nilda what are you talking about?"

Jesus and her mother quarrelled and fought almost daily now. Jesus returned late at night, and her mother left very early in the mornings, so she was the one who had to get her brothers and sisters off to school, before getting herself ready for school. In the evenings when she came home she had to cook dinner and get the younger ones to do their homework before their work-weary mother came home.

About a week earlier, her mother had beaten her, accusing her of having a boyfriend, a man much older than she was; that instead of going to school, Nilda was meeting this man at Cross Roads and they were going off together. She had denied it then, but really it was true. Between sobs, Nilda said, "I just wanted you to know I'm leaving. Going to live with Kirk."

"Kirk?"

"The man Mama was beating me about the other day."

"Nilda," I said, "don't do it."

She rolled her head from side to side. "Gloria, things not right in my house. The strain's too much. I can't take it any more."

"But Nilda, running away is not going to solve the problem!"

"It will! It will!" she stamped her feet as if she was trying to convince herself of this too. "Kirk, he has his own room. He says he will take care of me. We leaving Kingston. We going to another parish to live. Kirk will take care of me. Kirk will take care of everything."

"Where you going to live, Nilda, which parish, and for how long?"

"No," she shook her head, "Kirk tell me not to tell anybody. He says if I tell anybody, it will just ruin everything."

My mind was working overtime now, trying to think of all the reasons I'd heard older women give younger girls to discourage them from making moves like this one. I knew enough to know what she was doing was wrong. If I could find out where she was going I could tell her mother or the police where to look for her; or go to see her myself.

"For how long, Nilda?" Nilda was a fixture in my life. Someone besides whom I measured myself; measured my world. She'd always lived in the house in front of mine. She was my friend. I couldn't imagine her not being a part of my life.

"And what about school?" I asked, thinking this was a good solid question. She'd always liked school.

"I was never as bright as you. I could never get into a school like All Saints. Kirk says he'll take care of me, all I'll have to do is stay home and do whatever I please. I will cook and clean only if I want to. I can do without school." She was sobbing really hard now, a forlorn little girl desperately trying to convince herself that what she was doing was the best thing to do. I put an arm around her shoulder and gave her a hug. Finally, she hugged me back.

"I have to go," she said, her chest heaving. "Kirk's waiting."

"Nilda, please." I said, holding onto her. Now I was crying.

"It's for the best, Gloria. All my troubles will be taken care of. And if you're really my friend and want the best for me, you won't tell anyone you saw me tonight. You won't say anything at all. Please give me the chance I need." She gathered up her bag and I watched her struggle with it as she went behind Miss Christie's house towards the path, where she was soon swallowed up by the darkness.

I stood there, half hoping she would come back. Nilda and I had done so much together: played, teased and troubled each other endlessly, and now she was gone. I stood under the tamarind tree and wept. Later I thought I should have encouraged her to go and talk to Rachel. If there was anyone in the yard who could've talked to her, who could've talked some sense into her, it was Rachel. Why hadn't I thought of that?

Later in the night when panic struck Nilda's mother, I was in bed crying. At first Nadia started looking for her in the yard, saying she was going to beat Nilda within an inch of her life because she had no business being in people's house this late at night.

"Nilda? Nilda!" she shouted.

There was no answer. Nilda had been gone for hours.

She pounded on our door, asking if I'd seen Nilda. It must have been midnight by then. "Gloria you and Nilda close. You and Nilda good friends. Did you see her? Did she tell you anything?"

I shook my head.

Nadia dropped to the ground and started rolling around in the dirt. Despite how late it was, a crowd gathered, all the women shaking their heads and murmuring. No one, not even Miss Christie, had seen Nilda leave. Miss Christie kept eyeing me, shaking her head and saying, "These girl childrens. They can be such a disappointment, such a disappointment these girl children."

Mama and Rachel helped Nadia up and gave her some water to drink, to try and calm her down.

"Where is Jesus when I need him?" Nadia wailed.

On the steps of their house Nilda's four little brothers and sisters sat with blank stares on their faces. The child who followed Nilda, Nadine, was quietly crying. Nadia had discovered by then that all Nilda's clothes were missing. She vowed to find Nilda and give her the beating of a lifetime – and take her boyfriend to court for statutory rape.

The other women in the yard gathered around her with folded arms and clucked like worried hens, offering as much comfort as they could, before everyone started dispersing.

Back in my bed I hugged my pillow close and cried. No matter what I did the tears would not stop coming. Mama touched me and said, "Try to calm down, Gloria. Try to get some sleep."

I kept wondering if I would ever see Nilda again.

"Gloria," my mother said, "you wouldn't do anything that stupid would you?"

"No, Mama." I managed to say.

"That's my girl." She was straightening my pillow and fussing with my sheet. I could see she was trying to do something useful with her hands, they were trembling so badly.

"This yard," she said, "this yard is the cause of all of this problem. We have to get us out of this yard!"

I was still awake when Jesus stumbled home in the early hours of the morning. The quarrelling and fighting started immediately.

## CHAPTER 7

The next day at school I was in such a state that Annie threatened to take me to the guidance counsellor if I would not tell her what was wrong. I could barely get a word out. Tears kept sliding down my cheeks, despite my best efforts to stop them. Annie kept hold of my hand and would not let it go. Eventually I was able to tell her what had happened the night before, how Nilda had slipped off in the dark and out of my life.

At first Annie was speechless, even slightly overwhelmed by what I was saying. She looked as if for all her talk, her "scrapbook of atrocities", some of what happened on the island stayed beyond the reach of her life. Just then, the gulf between our lives, hers up on the hills with both her parents, chauffeur driven to school, helpers at her beck and call, and mine lived in the yard, could not have been wider. For a while it seemed too wide to cross and we were stranded on opposite sides of a river. For each of us, the river had a very different song.

"Honestly, Gloria," Annie said after a while, "I did not know things like that actually happened ... not here in Jamaica. I did not know that someone ... someone as young as Nilda ... would have to get herself and her brothers and sisters off to school in the mornings; would be responsible for so much. I have never ... I have never had to think about anything like this before."

I looked at her and had to smile. Despite all of our differences, we had somehow managed to find each other and start a friendship which had blossomed into something truly wonderful, like the golden yellow poui tree she often told me about in her back yard, when its flowers suddenly lit up the bare branches. It was a friendship I could not ever have imagined having; now I could not imagine being without it. Some of what I was feeling must have communicated to Annie because she squeezed my hand. Yes, I thought, looking at her, I had Annie, and Annie had me, and whatever else happened we would always have each other.

Before long Zekie was living with us. It wasn't anything official; he didn't immediately move his many possessions out of the hotel where he was staying into our house. It happened slowly, over the weeks, then months he and Mama were seeing each other. Slowly-slowly he became a regular part of the house, his clothes turning up in the tiny closet Mama and I shared, making it more cluttered. Now we were always getting into each other's way; in each other's face. The house was too small for the three of us. One of us would have to go and I was determined to do whatever I could do to make Zekie's stay as uncomfortable as possible.

Oh, how I disliked the man! What a pain he was! Always trying to talk to me! Always trying to find out what was going on with me! Space! He was taking up way too much space! What made it worse was that Zekie tolerated *me* well enough, was infuriatingly patient.

One day when I sat glaring at him, he waited until my mother had gone out to the standpipe.

"I don't know what the problem is you have with me, Gloria, and I don't know how I can fix it. But you need to understand something: I work long and hard to get your mother, *very long* and *very hard*. If you were a little older I would tell you just how long and just how hard – all the things I did in New York to try and forget her. Many other women. Still, no matter what I did, I could never forget her. Every night she was in my sleep and walking up and down in my head, your mother. I like you, Gloria, really I do, despite you behave so bad. Call me an idiot, but I like you and I more than like your mother. We have to find a way to get along, because, as far as your mother is concerned, I'm not about to lose her."

I stood looking at him, fire leaping from my eyes, my arms on my hips.

He held my stare, waiting for me to answer, before shrugging and turning away. "We can make this easy, or we can make this hard. You decide!"

Something I never fully understood happened at that moment, but I did not see it then. No, looking back now, I can see that it was then that the way I thought about him began to change. But it did not seem so at first. Then it only seemed that he, like me, was playing the deception game. When Mama was around, we were just the three most cheerful persons in the world. Eating, laughing, talking and joking. Anyone looking at us would have said, *Well, now, isn't that a wonderful family!* But when my mother was not around, it was a whole different story. Zekie and I took pains to avoid each other, keep out of each other's way. He kept on giving me gifts, a gold bracelet and a trip to an uptown restaurant for my thirteenth birthday, even talked of paying for braces for my teeth. But we continued circling each other, avoiding each other. Still, it bothered me that he did not work – and had all of that money. Where exactly did he get it from? Whenever I tried to talk to Mama about it, she would either try to convince me he was some kind of legitimate business man or she would tell me not-to-get-it-into-my-head-that-I-was-a-woman-now-getting-into-big-people's-business. Still I kept pressing her until she developed another tactic that she would henceforth stick to: Did I, did anyone, know exactly where those other people got their money from? Did I really know where the parents of my-good-friend-Annie, got their money from? She would leave the questions hanging in the air.

If the house was small before, it was cramped now, and with Zekie always around I could barely breathe. And if I resented the man because of this, I resented even more what my mother had become – a giant sky-blue butterfly hovering over a bright yellow flower.

They began talking about finding a bigger, better place to live. We each needed our own space, he said, giving me a fake little smile. Naturally, I gave him a fake little smile back. Whether my mother understood what was going on, the game we were playing, the pretty light-hearted butterfly said nothing. Actually, this is not quite true. She was pleased with herself, relieved at how Zekie and I seemed to be getting along. Now and again she spoke to me about Nilda's leaving. Wanting to make sure I would never do anything so stupid. Letting me know in so many ways Nilda would regret it.

One day I caught her looking at me in a way I had never seen before. Her eyes travelled up and down my skinny frame before settling on the mounds on my chest. Breasts. They had arrived quite suddenly, as if one morning I woke up and they were there, extra appendages on my body. I was still trying to adjust to them.

A few days later my mother came home and handed me a brown paper bag, in it two new lace brassieres. She said absolutely nothing to me about them, just left me to figure out how exactly to put them on. She was very silent after that and I sensed a new wariness in her eyes. That day I fumbled and fumbled with the brassiere until at last I got it on. Then I stared at myself in the mirror. I fingered the off white and shell-coloured lace. I viewed myself from the front and then turned to the side. I was almost there. I was becoming the thing called a woman.

Annie was changing too, literally stretching and growing before my very eyes. She was now a tall slender girl, with a tiny waist and full breasts. Bright red hair always gathered into two thick plaits, which hung like ropes at the side of her head. She still had many brown freckles on her pale face. She was a quick darting girl, a long-tailed iridescent hummingbird, always in motion, moving from place to place. She garnered much attention wherever she went.

Sometimes – I cannot lie – when we went out together, I couldn't stand how the boys would carry on over her, how they would look past me to her, my best friend, this most exotic of creatures. I complained about this once, saying that if I were as pale and red-haired, the boys would pay as much attention to me. Annie, good-natured Annie, just heard out my complaints, then took my face in her hands and said, "To me, Gloria, you are the most beautiful person in the world. I always wish I had your dark complexion!"

She brought her face close to mine, so close that for a moment I thought she was going to kiss me. But I saw that she was only looking at the reflection of herself in my eyes, and I looked for the reflection of myself in hers. But there again, curled up in their furthermost depths was the thing I could not name, the thing that seemed so far far away, the part of her that always seemed to be hiding. I came closer still, as if to reach a hand out to that hidden part of her; what I saw again was a girl holding herself and rocking, but as she'd done before, Annie laughed and pulled away. Still I could see that a troubling thought – perhaps even a dangerous thought – had entered her eyes.

"What is it?" I asked.

"Nothing."

I looked at her and snorted. "What is it?" I asked again.

Her face rumpled in a frown. A troubled and troubling look in her eyes. Oh how differently one sees things as one grows older! How clear things become from a certain distance! But even then I thought there was something very fragile, very vulnerable about Annie, something that could too easily fall apart.

Grafting and crossbreeding fruits and flowers was all the rage in Jamaica at that time. People would have several different types of one fruit – mangoes, for example – growing on one tree. And the flowers! People doing all sorts of amazing things with flowers! Double-fringed this! Triple-fringed that! Annie had a joke about these crossbred flowers. Yes, how spectacular they looked, she said, with a mocking laugh, but have you ever noticed, how easily, with the slightest touch, the smallest bit of wind, they tore and fell apart. Couldn't stand up to much at all. Didn't have the resistance of even the most common island flower. If she were a plant, she said one day when we were walking in the Botanical Gardens at Hope, she wanted to be something that could stand up to any weather. She did not want to be like the much prized shame-mi-lady flowers that, with one touch, curled tightly upon themselves and one had to wait and wait to see if they would ever reopen. These plants that everyone talks so much about, she said that day. Beautiful crossbred flowers!

"What is it?" I asked her yet again, and she hesitated a long time before she started talking.

"Gloria, promise me that we will be together. *Always*. I want us to always be friends."

"Of course we'll always be friends!" I laughed. "What in the world could ever keep us from being together!" I felt the same

99

strong bond between us as she did, the same need always to be close, and I could not understand why she should want me to make such a promise. She was what I heard one teacher describe as a kindred spirit, someone who completed me. After I told her all of these things the fire started burning in her eyes again. I saw the girl who delighted in breaking every possible rule. Always challenging the teachers ("But Mrs. Clarke ... you're wrong...! And why don't we have all these rules for boys! They should get kicked out of school too if they get a girl pregnant!... But Mrs. Jones, how could that be so!").

"Yes Gloria," she said as we locked arms, "we will always and always be the best of friends!"

Now that I had breasts the boys and men around the yard began paying me closer attention. The boys my age I could handle; they were never that forthright, and all I had to do was give them a good tracing-out. It was the older men, like Ageable and God-is-Love, who left me confused and distressed – men who had known me since I was a child running-up-and-down-in-the-yard; men who had held my hand and taken me across the street; men whose women and baby mothers I knew.

Once a man whistled at me when Nadia and I were at the standpipe. It was too much for Nadia who flew into a rage and gave the man a good cursing out.

"You don't see she is still a child? Just a little girl? What is the matter with you grown men anyway? You can't find a woman your own age to whistle at, you whistling at this little girl?" She was frustrated. Nilda had been gone for months and no one had heard anything. Even though Nadia had reported her missing to the police and checked with them almost daily, nothing had turned up. She'd been forced to cut back her hours of work, so she could get the younger children off to school in the mornings, and she was beginning to feel the pinch. She rarely had enough lunch money for all four of them, and some mornings, when it was all too much for her, she would blast Nilda for leaving.

"Such an ungrateful, ungrateful wretch! I wish terrible things on her! Selfish little wretch! How could she leave me in this state? No one to help me with the children! Certainly not that no-good father of hers, who can't even find his way to his yard come night any more! I hope that man, Kirk, whatever his real name is, give her everything she looking for! Everything she looking for and more!"

But other times I heard her sobbing, asking the Lord to return her child to her unharmed.

Jesus was now gone for days at a time and when he did come home he was usually drunk. Before Nilda left, Jesus was not any kind of drinker and, even if late, he would always come home. Despite his other women, he still came home every night. Now it seemed as if coming home was too painful for him, but no one told him they were sorry about what had happened with Nilda. He was a man and a man did not need that kind of comfort. Indeed, when Nilda's name came up in conversation, he talked as if he didn't care. "If she wants to go live with a man and leave her family behind, well let her go!"

But I could see through the bravado and rum-talk that Nilda's disappearance had touched him to the core, and I wished I could tell her what her leaving had done to her family, done to the yard. Nothing was the same since she left. A sullen mood had settled over the entire place. Her younger brothers and sisters were the ones who felt it most, from the looks in their dark brown eyes, they couldn't make heads or tails of what was going on around them. They dearly missed their older sister and the stability she provided. What little structure Nilda had given their house was rapidly collapsing.

Now Nadia was training Nadine, the child who followed Nilda, to take on some of the household responsibilities. One day I watched as she struggled with some washing and tried to get the younger ones to do their homework. Already she was developing the dejected stoop of her older sister. I didn't want to think about what would eventually happen.

Nilda's disappearance had also made its mark on Mama. All she talked about was getting a place and moving out of the yard. For her, the yard itself was the problem. It was as if the yard got its claws into you, never to let you go, Mama kept saying. And as Miss Sarah often said, few of the people who moved into the yard, ever moved out unless it was in a pine box. Mama was determined she would be one of those who actually did move out and not in a coffin. With Zekie she was convinced they could do it. She diligently searched the housing section of the *Gleaner* every Sunday, looking for somewhere "nice" that she and Zekie could afford. If they could not make it up to the hills, then Constant Spring, at the foot of the hills, was good enough for her. She enlisted Zekie in her cause.

"This is not a place to live and to bring up your children," she said to him. "Look what happen to Nilda. And she was a real nice child, that Nilda. And Denise, feisty though she was, look what happen to her. I know Gloria would never do anything so stupid, but I still want to get her out of this yard." Usually when Mama talked about moving, she would look over at me for reassurance. Just the fact that I was there, in the house with her, and not outside in the yard keeping company with God-knows-who was enough to comfort her. She now strictly forbade me to be outside after dark.

Zekie agreed. He even joked with Mama that perhaps they should get married, make the family official. In his joking, however, there was a serious edge and I knew he really wanted to marry her. *That* for him would be a dream come true. He no longer talked of going back to America. In fact, it seemed he could not put enough space between himself and New York. People even began to say something terrible must have happened in New York. Something he was desperately trying to get away from.

Now, when Mama asked him about New York, he would shrug his shoulders and say America was never a place where he wanted to spend the rest of his life. He'd got what he'd wanted to get in America, and now was content to make his life in Jamaica. I did not believe this, and he knew that I did not believe it, but neither of us said anything about it to the other. He had long given up trying to win me over, and, knowing this, for some strange reason I began to accept him. At first a little. Then more and more. I was still, and would always be, bothered by how he made his money, but what could I do? He had made it clear that he was not going to get out of my mother's life, and since I would always be a part of it, I reasoned I might as well get used to the idea that he was going to be around. Even when I was still scheming to get him out, I'd had to admit that our life had gotten so much better since he'd come. And there were little things he did for my mother that took my breath away. Like the time he was late coming home. Mama had spent hours preparing dinner and was fuming.

"I'm sorry, I'm sorry," he kept calling all the way from the gate! When he came in he handed her a pink gift bag and a bunch of roses – the words "Just For You" written on a card.

"What is this?" Mama asked, looking at the bag and trying not to smile at the man who had kept her waiting so long.

"Just open the bag!"

There was a new make-up kit inside.

"I know you love your make up. I spent hours looking for this."

Mama opened up the kit. So many colours! And three different sections to the kit! She pulled out one section, looked at it for a while, before she burst out laughing.

"What's so funny?" Zekie asked, looking a little hurt.

"These foundation colours are not my colours, but not to worry, my darling, I will wear the lip gloss and eye shadow!"

Even I joined in the laughter. Zekie looked at me and I just kept laughing and laughing.

"Men!" my mother said to me later that night. But this time she said it differently – with something like a caress in her voice. And this time, what she had to say and the way she said it did not get on my last nerve.

It was Saturday morning and I was up early mopping the veran-dah, before getting ready to head off to the library where I would meet Annie, as I did every Saturday now. Zekie would be driving Mama to the market in downtown Kingston and I couldn't wait for them to leave so I could have the place to myself. Then I could change into and out of as many outfits as I wanted without having to hear Mama go on and on about how she could not understand what-was-really-going-on-at-that-library-on-Tom-Redcam-Av-enue-you-have-to-change-your-clothes-so-many-times!

I decided to pass the time until they left by taking a long warm bath, and from the bathroom I listened to Mama and Zekie having breakfast. Zekie was telling Mama a joke and she was laughing so hard she was having difficulty catching her breath. I soaped and re-soaped myself, until my skin glowed. I knew I really should come out of the bathroom, but I wanted them to leave first.

"Do you plan to stay in that bathroom forever?" Mama shouted.

"No, not forever."

"But just until I leave! Think I don't know what you're up to!" From her voice I could tell she was in a good mood.

"Up to?" I pretended I didn't understand what she was talking about.

"I was your age once, and it was not that long ago. I know all about dressing up and going to the library. I know what you young people get up to!"

I laughed and did not answer her.

A couple of minutes later, she shouted, "I'm off to the market. I'll see you this evening when you come home from the library. And don't stay too late there. Tell Annie hello for me!"

I waited until I heard the door close before I came out of the bathroom, with a towel wrapped around me. I sat down at the table and ate my breakfast of fried plantains and hot cocoa. Oh, how I loved having the house all to myself! I undid the towel and stared at myself for a long time, at my very long legs, my thin shoulders and arms, my round breasts, and the slight curve of my hips. I reached for the lotion and started rubbing it onto my arms and legs. After the lotion I added powder, deodorant, and, finally, a few drops of Mama's expensive new perfume. I stood there still looking at myself in the mirror. Frowning at some things; nodding at others. I don't know how long I'd been naked in front of the mirror when I had the uncomfortable feeling that I was being watched. I looked up and there was Jesus looking at me through the window; he stood there just watching me. I did not know quite how to read the expression on his face, in his eyes, for his eyes seemed to have no soul in them, and he look tired, defeated, sad. A little drunk. He seemed to be looking past me to something else in the room that only he could see. Perhaps he was searching the room for his daughter Nilda.

I let out a panicked scream and reached for the towel. I gathered up the clothes I'd finally settled on wearing and ran into the bathroom to put them on. My heart was racing wildly as I dressed. How long had he been standing there? What did he think he was doing? When I came back out of the bathroom, he was gone. I sat in silence for a long time, thinking. Why would Jesus do such a thing? He had never done anything like this before. He was not one of the men around the yard who were now bothering me. Why would he do such a thing? I was shaking so hard I felt my knees would buckle. I looked down at myself and was instantly ashamed of my body. If it hadn't been for these breasts, for the hips that had rounded out, then no one would be looking at me, no one would be paying me this kind of attention, no one would be whistling or passing notes to me. I wished I could push them back, my breasts, have them reabsorbed into my body. I started shaking so hard I had to hold onto the table for support. Suddenly the house was too small, too hot and too stuffy. I had to get outside very quickly or I would faint. I gathered up the things I was taking to the library with me and hurried outside. Once outside I ran all the way to the library.

That evening when I came home, Mama was in her own little world of herbs and spices, cooking dinner. She turned, smiled and nodded at me when I came through the door.

"How was the library today? Got *any* work done?" she teased, still in a very good mood.

"Yes. I did get some work done."

"And how is Annie?"

"She's fine. She asked me about coming to visit her again this weekend."

Instead of getting angry about this, as she usually did, Mama did something totally unexpected: she smiled at me and my question and was not in the least bit annoyed.

"Well," she said, looking up at me from her pot, "if we move from here to somewhere better, somewhere like Constant Springs, well then, you just might be able to go and visit. And guess what?" she added in a conspiratorial whisper, "Annie just might be able to visit back."

I wanted to talk to her, tell her what had happened this morning with Jesus, but she was in such a good mood that I didn't want to spoil it. It would be another secret I would have to keep. Something else to put in the unlined box in the storage closet of my chest where I had put so many things lately.

I put down my bag and went to sit by myself on the verandah. The flowers of the hibiscus that only a few days before had been in full bloom were now wilting in the scorching hot sun. I reached over and touched one and the petals fell off. I crushed the petals between my fingers and they squirted a liquid that looked like blood all over my hands. I did not like how the flowers looked now that they had all wilted. It seemed as if they had somehow done something wrong; were somehow at fault. They seemed to be hanging their heads in shame.

## CHAPTER 8

How quickly the year came and went at All Saints! The last day of the school year came, and Annie and I had to say goodbye to each other for the long months of summer. I did not know how I would manage not seeing her. She was going to visit relatives in Canada, and I was reluctantly going to stay with Grandy. We sat outside, under the shade of the lignum vitae trees, neither of us saying much. Since it was the last day of school, there were no formal classes.

"And not once did you come to visit me!" Annie said, pouting slightly.

"You know I would've come if I could. You know what my mother has to say about it."

"Still..." And we both knew she was insisting just to insist.

"You know I'm going to miss you," I said quietly.

"And I'm going to miss you too." She hung her head so I would not see her bottom lip trembling and the tears beginning in her dark green eyes.

"Well, let's look on the bright side. At least we're out of Mrs. Clarke's class!"

"Thank goodness for that!" Annie shuddered. "I don't think she could stand yet another, 'but Mrs. Clarke!' from me."

"No, I don't think she could." And we both burst out laughing.

"I'll write to you from Canada," Annie looked down at the piece of paper on which I'd written my grandmother's address.

"And I'll write back. I wish I was going to Canada with you."

"One day, one day, you and me together Gloria, we're going to do a lot of travelling!"

"One day, one day." I replied.

Before leaving for Lluidas Vale, I went to see Rachel. She was feeling much better and was up and about her room and outside in the yard. Her room was back to tiptop shape, and she was again the woman who wielded much power in the yard. The doctor she was now seeing, a private doctor, had given her medication that was helping tremendously. She also confessed to me one day that she'd gone to see a "man", who told her there was nothing but spirits bothering her. For the right price, he could rid her of them. She'd paid him handsomely.

My eyes bulged when Rachel told me this; she was the woman who used to scoff at such things, who thought obeahmen were scamps parting people from their hard-earned money.

Rachel looked shamefaced, when she saw the look on my face.

"Gloria," she said after a while, "sometimes a body gets desperate. Sometimes a body gets tired. Life is hard, true, but sweet, too. No one ever come back from the other side yet to tell me things any better over there than how we have it here. You save yourself any way you can."

She was right of course. If I'd been in her position, wouldn't I have done just about anything to save myself?

"So you going to the country," she said, after a while.

I nodded. For the first time ever I would be going by myself. Grandy could not come and get me because of her arthritis and Mama could not get the time off work to take me, so I would board the bus in the depot in downtown Kingston and go to Lluidas Vale by myself. Grandy was mortified when she heard the news; she still thought of me as her baby, the one in the pink and white blanket she'd picked up from Jubilee Hospital when you-were-no-bigger-than-the-palm-of-my-hand. I was certain I was old enough to get to Lluidas Vale by myself, to find my way to the house in the blue Portland mountains.

Rachel looked hard at me. I hadn't answered her question directly.

"Yes," I finally replied. "I'll be going to the country."

"So why you sound like that?"

"Oh, I don't know," I said, throwing up my hands and wanting to change the subject, but Rachel knew me too well. She just waited for me to go on, and finally I did. "I just wish I could do something different this summer, like go away. Like go some place different. Like go to Canada ..." It seemed to me everyone at All Saints was going abroad for the summer. We were sitting outside, under the shade of the tamarind tree. A small wind was playing with the fallen leaves in the yard, turning them this way, then that, before sweeping them in a frenzy off the ground. I watched as they tried to settle, but the wind was relentless, always stirring them up, never giving them a chance to settle down.

"I know you wish you going somewhere else, but for now, going to see your grandmother in the country not all that bad," Rachel shoved me playfully. "And I promise you, as sure as I sitting here on this old tree stump, one day you will get to do all the travelling in the world you want to do. Just you pay attention to your books."

I gave a sheepish grin. Rachel divided the world into two spheres: those who went to school and those who did not. For those who went to school, the world was for their taking. For the rest ...

"Try to enjoy yourself this summer," she chided. "And say hello to your grandmother for me, even though we both know she don't like me."

"I will. I will tell her hello. And who says she doesn't like you?"

Rachel looked at me without answering.

Later that evening while I was packing, I shuddered when I came across the pink dress I'd made such a fuss about last year. It looked so childish, so out of step with what everyone at All Saints was wearing. Mama could not get me near that dress even if she paid me to wear it. It was in any case too short and too tight for me now, with all the rambunctiousness going on with my body. "Give it to Nadia for her one of daughters," I said to Mama, tossing the dress onto the growing pile of clothes on the bed I would not be taking with me.

Mama winced when I threw the dress down, and rushed over to pick it up. She held it tenderly in her arms, as if she were holding a baby. She ran her fingers over the sequins on the front of the dress and straightened out the bow at the back. Last year, she had berated me when I came back with it from the country and had searched and searched it, surprised not to find not-even-one-itty-bitty-stain. She continued looking down at the dress.

"I might as well give it away," she said. "It don't look like you have any plans of ever wearing it again. Yes," she continued after a while, "I'll give it to Nadia for one of her girls."

The next day Mama accompanied me to the bus depot in Kingston. At the depot she and I hugged and kissed each other. I was almost as tall as she was now. After a while we just stood there, looking at each other. She looked bereft, as if there were so many things she wanted to tell me, so much left unsaid, but she did not know where to begin.

"Remember to give everyone my love," she said, as I climbed into the bus. I kept thinking about the look on her face, a combination of love, pride, and some emotion I could not name. What was happening between my mother and me? Why did she act as though she didn't want me to go on the bus by myself, but, in the end almost pushed me in? Why did she have such a pitiful, mournful look on her face? Was she crying or was I just imagining things? On the long ride to Lluidas Vale I had plenty of time for such questions.

And of course I could not make head nor tail of my own emotions. How I wanted her to let me go – she seemed to have so many arms entangling me. But when she stepped back, how I longed for her. More and more I found myself looking at her and seeing her looking at me. As if in a looking glass, I kept thinking. As if in a looking glass.

"Gloria! Gloria, over here!" I heard someone shouting as soon as I got off the bus several hours later in Port Antonio Bay. It was my old friend Monique. But what a different Monique! Last summer we were both at the same eye level, now she had shot past me and had a tall gangly body she seemed desperate to control. An old excitement started bubbling up inside me as soon as I saw her.

"Gloria!" Monique came running up. "I wasn't sure it was you standing there. I finagled my mother into taking me with her to the Bay, because I just knew you would be coming today. It's so good to see you!" she gave me a hug and reached over and grabbed one of my bags.

"Oh no, let's get a cart." I started looking around for one of the cart boys I could pay to drag my bags to the bus up to Lluidas Vale.

"A what?" Monique asked, pushing me and laughing. "I guess you have money to throw to the winds, talking about getting a cart when we only going just around the corner!"

"Your just-around-the-corner might be ten miles away!" I could not believe how good it was to see her! I could not believe I had not wanted to come to the country!

I was struggling with one heavy bag, trying to keep up with and talk to Monique, when I heard a voice I would recognize anywhere. A voice I so dearly loved! A voice I always carried around in my head. Grandy's voice! She was talking to someone who was laughing and laughing. I stood still for a moment and just listened to her talk before I hurried around the corner to where she was. She saw me at the exact moment I saw her.

"Is that my Glory?" Grandy said, getting up from where she was sitting outside a restaurant, "Is that my Glory?" She was wearing a multi-coloured dress with a white cap pulled close over her head to keep the sun off her face. She was sitting beside a woman whom I recognized as one of her church sisters, bone-deep in some conversation. Now the woman was immediately forgotten.

My fingers itched to touch the soft folds of my grandmother's face. I wanted to bury my face in her shoulder, and inhale the rich earthy smell peculiarly her own. I wanted to rub my face against her face as I'd done since you-were-a-baby-no-bigger-than-the-palm-of-my-hand. I wanted her to wrap her fat warm arms around me and hold me close.

"Is that my Gloria?" She opened wide her arms, and I dropped my bag where I was and ran straight into them.

"Look my trouble!" Grandy was smiling at me in her arms, "This girl so big now, she almost knock me over! This child almost too big now for my own hands! Just you look my trouble." She turned to the woman beside her, pointing at me and laughing.

"She has grown in truth," the woman said. "Quite nice and lovely. Much bigger than she was last year. How these children does grow! Child, how is your mother?" She cocked her head to the side, wanting to know.

"She's doing just fine," I said, untangling myself from my grandmother. She always had that effect on me and no matter how much I pretended I was above running to her, no matter how much I promised myself to stop behaving like a child, I always ended up running straight into her arms and nuzzling my head into the side of her neck.

"I hear she find herself a nice gentleman-fellow to settle down with," the woman winked at Grandy, and they both burst out laughing.

"Delroy," my grandmother called to one of the men sitting on the piazza, "get Gloria bags for me. Come Monique, both you and Gloria come into the restaurant out of the sun and get something cool to drink and a bite to eat. You all have to eat fast, because it's soon time for the bus to come and take us up to the district."

From the start there was something very different about this holiday. For one thing Yvette was no longer living in the district, and I couldn't help but be disappointed by this. Yvette's absence made a hole; our group was just not the same without her. It was as if its very soul had been taken out.

"That child," Grandy said, shaking her head when I asked about her, "God only knows what is going to become of her. The last time she was here, she didn't look too good. She didn't seem herself ... Oh, I can't put my finger on it ... But you could see the child look sad. She wasn't too happy. Her mother, that girl, she needs her mother."

It began, Grandy said, when Yvette came to visit during the middle of the school year and stayed with her father for weeks on end, when she should've been in school with her aunt in Montego Bay. Yvette seemed troubled, wandering about the place, as if she was looking for something. When anyone tried to talk to her, she would either tell them to mind their own goddamn business, or she would just burst into tears. It got so people were afraid to talk to her, because they didn't know which way her breeze would blow.

One time, Grandy said, Yvette came to visit and both of them sat outside on the verandah for the longest time, drinking lemonade. At first, Yvette just sat there, but after a while she began to talk, asking Grandy what she thought had really happened to her mother, whether she thought she'd really died in New York, telling Grandy she didn't even have a picture of her.

Grandy told her that her mother was a woman who loved flowers, who adored oleanders and periwinkles, a woman who painted the little house they lived in a bright aquamarine blue – which had faded over the years to a kind of teal-green colour, a woman who lined the walk from the street up to her house with smooth white stones she'd taken from the belly of the river. Always kept a parrot or some other colourful bird around her. But Grandy could not bring herself to tell Yvette that her mother was much too young for her father, that no one ever knew where her father had found such a young girl to set up house with so deep in the country. Grandy had not told Yvette that her mother always had sad eyes, how she would come every evening to the window to watch the big country bus which passed through the district just twice a day. Grandy had not told her about the times her mother had run away, and her father found her and dragged her back to the fading blue house in the country. "No," Grandy said, "I did not think it for the best to tell her all of that."

"Don't you miss Yvette?" I asked Junie, one day, when we were sitting outside on the verandah.

"Every day."

"When was the last time you saw her?" I wanted to get as much information about Yvette as I could.

"A few months back." Junie answered uncertainly.

"And?"

"She was alright … except she was sad in a way …"

"And?"

"And nothing else!" she snapped. "Her father and brothers, they moved away now, they no longer live around here, so I can't tell you what happened to Yvette." She sounded as if this was something she was still trying to deal with.

Thinking about Yvette's departure I felt the same powerlessness and hopelessness as when Nilda left. Someone else had moved out of my life, someone else I did not know if I would ever see again. I found myself very close to tears. What I really wanted to know, what I really wanted to ask my grandmother, Monique and Junie, but could not ask, was whether Yvette had asked about me, had wondered about me, as I found myself wondering about her almost every day. When, if ever would I see her again?

Now I found that our mothers and grandmothers were insisting we stay closer to home, saying we were becoming young women now and it was time we stopped wandering about, going into other people's yards. They fussed about the way we "carried ourselves", the clothes we wore, whether or not we had slippers on our feet and tie-heads on our heads. We were constantly told to stay away from boys and try and be "decent". Even Grandy joined in, saying it did not look proper my going to "everyone's" yard. She wasn't telling me I could not visit my friends, she insisted, but not nearly as often, and I should let the other girls do the visiting sometimes, and there were yards I should avoid.

During the day I took Uncle Silas's breakfast and lunch to him. It was plain to see he was getting old and tired and couldn't take care of his field as he used to, but was making a valiant effort at keeping everything up. Now Grandy was bothering him about selling off some of his land, giving up some of his responsibilities. She knew he would always keep some land, for he was the kind of man who always had to have something to do with his ten green fingers, but he could not possibly handle all the acres he still had. Of course he disagreed with her, and kept refusing to sell his land. He was so tired that when he came for dinner in the evenings he would slump in the chair after eating and promptly fall asleep.

I found myself spending most of the time with Grandy. One night I sat on the grass in the yard, inhaling the stink-sweet smell of a bearing jackfruit tree, fireflies dancing all around me, alternately glowing, then going dark again. Grandy always said fireflies carried magic inside themselves, and if we caught one of them in our hands, then just for a moment we were holding magic. I tried catching a few, but they were too fast for me. Grandy was on the verandah sewing some curtains. Uncle Silas had already gone home after dinner, complaining about neck and backaches and needing to rest. Earlier in the week Grandy received a letter from Mama, telling her that she and Zekie had seen a house they were thinking of buying. Mama was very excited; the sooner we moved out of the yard the better. When Grandy told me about this new development I said nothing. I could feel her eyes on me, watching me, as if she was trying to make up her mind about something. She put down the curtains and came to sit on the grass next to me. The night was cool and the sky was ink-blue with fat silver stars. She pulled her legs up under her as if she was a young girl, my grandmother.

"You know," she said, staring up in the sky, "if you ever see one of those stars falling out of the sky, you should make a wish. If you don't tell anyone about the wish, then it will come true."

"I know," I said, for she had told me this several times before.

"And what would you wish for?" She asked what should have been an innocent question, but I knew it was not.

"If I told you it wouldn't come true!" I protested.

"But there are no stars falling from the sky."

"Not yet."

"And do you want a star to fall from the sky tonight?"

From this question I knew things were getting serious. There was something she wanted to find out. She knew something about the letter was bothering me, and she wanted to know what it was.

"I don't know," I replied, hanging my head down.

"Gloria," she took my arm into hers, " you want to talk to me about something?"

I did not feel like talking. I just wanted to lie on my back in the grass watching the fireflies.

"Why don't you like Zekie?" she finally asked directly, waiting patiently for an answer. When she didn't get one, she continued, "You don't want to see your mother happy? You don't want to see her with someone? Go on, tell your Grandy."

Still I kept quiet.

"You know, when I was a girl, young like you, my mother told me a story. Yes," she continued, smiling, "my mother who died long before you were born told me this story about a girl, young like you, who used to keep secrets. Unnecessary secrets. In the end one of those secrets cost her her life. This girl, she was beautiful in every way: eyes as bright as a morning star, nice lips, and just the most perfect figure in the world. All the mens wanted her, and they did all sorts of things to get her attention: took her the biggest and ripest plantains and bananas; sent her bucket loads of ripe yellow guavas; the mens did just about anything to get her, but not one of them ever succeeded. You see, after a while that girl start believing she perfect, too good for anyone. She spent hours just looking at her reflection in whatever mirror she could find, but most of all she spent her time looking at herself in the biggest mirror of them all, the mirror of the river.

"One day while she busy admiring herself, a nasty little crawfish who'd been watching her do this for the longest time, decided he'd had enough of this girl and her beauty and vowed to teach her a lesson. He climbed up out of the river and, while she was still looking at herself in the water, pierced the sole of her foot and bored deep into her leg. Of course, the show-off girl was horrified! Couldn't believe something as old and ugly as a nasty crawfish had taken up residence in her body, and so, instead of telling her mother and all those around her what happened, she kept quiet about it. Kept this a secret. And the crawfish grew more and more every day, and soon her leg started to swell, then to fester and to stink, and still the girl refuse to talk, refuse to let the people around her know something as ugly as a crawfish was growing inside her body. You know what happen? Eventually she lost her leg, that girl, and soon after that, her life. So you see, Gloria, it's never a good thing to keep something in, to let it fester and grow inside you; it's always best to let things out."

I sighed. "Well, he really tries to be nice to me, Zekie does," I began. "Always buying me things, giving me things ... He's always buying Mama things. And he really isn't a bad man. I'm even beginning to like him. But there is all this money and I never see him working." I paused for a while, before continuing. "This really bothers me, Grandy, has always bothered me, and some-times when I try to talk to Mama about it she tells me that I-should-mind-my-own-business; and, if I think-I'm-some-kind-of-big-woman-now. Or, she does this thing of asking me if I know where all the other people with money get *their* money from." I closed my eyes. "Grandy it bothers me so. How he doles out money to the boys on the street corners; how he doles out money to Mama and even tries giving more and more of it to me.

All the things we now have. I try to tell myself I'm not taking the money I get directly from him – try to tell myself that I'm only taking money from Mama – but deep down I know better. Deep down I know where all this money is coming from, and Grandy, even though I can't do a thing about it, it still bothers me so!" I opened my eyes.

"I see." Grandy stayed quiet for a long time, thinking. After a while she got to her feet to go inside the house. "Let's hope your mother knows what she's doing; what she's getting herself into. It's getting late, we should go inside."

Yes, it was getting late and we should go inside, but I liked the feel of the night on my skin. The night in the country had a feel it did not have in the city. The darkness felt like a sheer smooth material that passed right through your hands. Lately, I found myself dreaming of wearing night around me, a sheer purple dress, which would flow behind me as I walked. Then I would become the night woman, with silver stars in my hair. Suddenly, a brilliant silver-star started falling from the sky.

"Quick!" Grandy pointed at the star before closing her eyes tight. "Make a wish, make a wish quick, Gloria! Look we just talking about it, and now we have a falling star! Make your wish now, Gloria." Her eyes were closed tight and she seemed to be concentrating hard on her wish. I decided to make a wish too and closed my eyes. When I opened them again, the star had disappeared. "What did you wish for?" I asked Grandy.

"Now you *know* I can't tell you that." She reached out a hand and helped me up from the grass. "And you can't tell me your wish either, or it won't come true."

Grandy did not need to tell me what she wished for: the worry lines creasing her forehead even deeper, and the look in her eyes after I told her about Zekie, was enough to let me know what she was wishing for. She was praying everything would work out well for Mama, that Zekie would not turn out to be who I thought he was. In a way, we both had the same wish.

Junie was in her yard tending to the flowers in her garden when I went to visit her the next day. She came to meet me at the gate, leaning against the large breadfruit tree as we chatted. Like

Monique, she had grown – though not as much as Monique – and not only in size, for there was a new maturity about her. "We haven't seen as much of each other as we should," I said, by a way of explanation of why I had called.

"Yes," she agreed, listlessly. "We haven't seen as much of each other as we usually do." She was quiet for a while, before she said: "Sometimes I wish I could go away and leave this place. Go somewhere else. I'm tired of all this greenery, all these bushes."

"And where would you go?" I was surprised: behind her the garden was in full bloom, and, to my eyes, it was the most well-tended garden I'd even seen.

"Anywhere else. Anywhere but here. Kingston, maybe."

"Kingston?" I laughed. "Kingston is not *all that* you know."

She shrugged. "Well, at least I would know what somewhere else was like."

"And who would tend your garden?" I motioned to the oval-shaped patch in front of her parent's house. "Just who would take care of your precious flowers?" There were tall red gingers, hibiscus flowers, Joseph-coats and white and blue morning glories.

"The garden can take care of itself!"

"Oh no!" I said, "the garden needs you to take care of it!"

Suddenly I doubled over as a piercing pain shot through me, a pain I'd never felt before. All morning long my stomach had been hurting me in a new way. I could not understand why it was cramping so badly. Before I knew what was happening my underwear felt warm and wet, as if something was crawling between my legs. I jumped to my feet and started shaking out my clothes.

"What is it?" Junie asked, frightened.

"I don't know, but there's something strange going on. I have to use your bathroom!"

"Come!" Junie said, and we took off, running. I ran faster and faster, because whatever was happening was spreading faster. Inside the bathroom, I lifted up my dress and both Junie and I stared. There was a large crimson stain on my underwear.

We both knew this day would come, but it was still a surprise. Up until now this day had been an abstraction. Something that would happen in a very distant future. The *it* my mother, my grandmother, even the nuns at school had told me about. The *it* both Annie and I had read so much about. Yes, I knew what was happening, that *it* had finally arrived, yet I still felt unprepared. I looked over at Junie whose eyes were as wide as saucers.

"I'm going to get my mother," she said, backing out of the room.

Time felt as if it was standing still. Perhaps I did not want time to move, for I knew from this day forward, my life would never be the same again. I felt pushed, not so much pushed as dragged, head to toe, from one stage of my life into another. I was frightened and felt very alone. Vaguely I heard Junie's mother talking to me, telling me everything would be alright; she knew from the look on my face this was my first time. Her voice sounded muffled, as if it was coming up to me from the bottom of a well. Tenderly, she guided me through the intricacies of putting on a napkin, how to fix it so it would not chafe my legs. I looked at her as if I was seeing her for the first time. It was hard to believe that this woman who planted and tended yams, dasheen, sweet potatoes, and coco, who could slaughter a pig or goat with a cutlass in those same hands, went through this too. Every cramp sent me reeling in a new direction, reaching for answers I did not have. The world seemed one huge multi-coloured prism that I was trapped in.

"You a woman now," Miss Marylee said, bringing me back to the moment, the sanitary napkin between my legs.

"No," I said, pulling away from her and feeling my way out of the bathroom, the napkin uncomfortable in my underwear. "No," I kept saying, shaking my head from side to side. This could not be true. This could not be happening. Miss Marylee was hanging something so huge on me, this word *woman*, that I would never be able to manage it and carry it around. She was hanging on me, it felt, the weight of the world. This word – *woman* – Mama had for years told me I was not, that Grandy had warned me against becoming before my time, that had resulted in Denise having a child. This word – *woman* – would be too much for me to carry around for the rest of my life. No, I said, backing away from both of them, as if I were a trapped animal trying to escape from a pen, this woman thing could not be happening to me right now. In my head I heard anew the words of a song the women often sung when they worked together, shelling peas or cutting bananas or canes. The words never made sense until now.

*Elena and she mumma go a market*
*Elena start bawl for she belly*
*Go home Elena, go home Elena*
*Go boil cerasee for you belly.*

Finally I understood why Elena's belly hurt. I edged past Junie and her mother until I found myself outside, and then I ran all the way home to Grandy. Somehow, even before I found the words to tell her what had happened, Grandy knew. From the look on my face, she knew. "It's OK. It's OK.," she kept saying, taking me in her arms. "It will be alright; just you sit down here and calm yourself."

I was sobbing. What would this mean for me now?

"Sit here and calm yourself, it's OK. Happen to every woman. In fact," she added with a sly grin, "there will be days when you long for it to happen. Just you sit here and try to calm yourself."

She went into the kitchen and came back out a few minutes later with a steaming cup of cerasee tea. "Here, it bitter and taste bad but drink this. It will calm you down and it will help with the pain."

I kept looking down at myself. Why was this body always betraying me?

"Course you know," Grandy was saying after I had calmed down a bit, "... you can make baby now, and we hope you don't do anything foolish and get yourself into trouble. We going have to clamp down on you more now. Keep you closer at home. You going have to be careful and watch out for those boys! Don't be foolish like your mother." She paused after saying this, before continuing, "But somehow I know you too smart to get yourself into that kind of trouble. You too smart to let some boy turn you into idiot. You see what happen to your mother, right?"

I nodded my head.

"We really can't have *that* happening to you, right?"

Again I nodded my head.

"Now that's a good girl. Go now and try to get some sleep."

It felt as though the ground I had been walking on for all the years of my life was breaking up beneath me. Everywhere there was a fracture and I was unsure where next to place my feet. If I made one wrong move, I would be swallowed up by some large dark thing. I got up and went to my room, thinking that perhaps when I woke up my life would be back to where it had been this morning, that perhaps when I woke up none of this would be happening.

## CHAPTER 9

"Of course you know you're a big girl now," my mother was saying to me, when I got back home at the end of the summer. "Now you know you have to be careful and don't do anything stupid." Grandy had written to her telling her I'd started menstruating.

"Yes, I know. Grandy already had *that* discussion with me."

"I bet she did," Mama said, laughing despite herself, "I bet she did! But as your mother, I just want to say my piece. Don't do anything foolish. Anything at all. Promise?"

"I promise."

"That's my girl," she patted my hand.

"Mama," I said, wanting to change the subject, "how is Rachel doing?" I had been home for several days and I hadn't seen her about the yard, and her room, when I went there, was locked. I must have caught my mother off guard with the question, because she looked as if she was sorry I mentioned the woman who for years had been her friend.

"In the hospital," she answered offhandedly, turning away from me. "She'll be home tomorrow, they say." Mama walked over to the new wall-unit in the ever more cramped space of the living room and started fiddling with her collection of figurines.

"Gloria, I need to tell you something now that you are growing up ... I know you have strong feelings for Rachel and I know you've seen that ... Rachel and I ... well, that we have been friends. But Ma Louise was right about Rachel ... she is not the type of person ... how should I put this? Rachel is not the type of person you – or I for that matter – should be keeping company with. She is not ... Oh Gloria ... I want you to think twice about your friendship with Rachel."

It took a while for what my mother was saying to sink in, and once it did I started backing away from her. If she wanted to turn her back on Rachel that was her business, but Rachel was my friend. Yes, I knew and was sorry about what she did "for a living", but that did not stop me loving her. I could not turn my back on her, especially now when she seemed to be getting sicker and sicker, when she was going to need more help. Even if my mother were to forbid it, I was still going to be friends with Rachel. I remembered all the talks I'd had with her after Nilda left. How Rachel had told me that when she was younger, she'd gotten pregnant for a man who discarded her like some rag he wiped his foot with as soon as he found out she was pregnant and intended to keep the baby. After the man left, she did not know what else to do but continue working the streets where this man had put her to work, along with other young girls from the country. She'd continued working the streets almost until she gave birth to the baby. The day she had her daughter, Rachel said she laboured hard and laboured long, but most of all she'd laboured alone. Unlike the other women on the ward, she had no visitors. When she finally had her baby, and the nurses cleaned her daughter up and brought the child back to her, she'd held the infant for a long-long time. The little girl was perfect, she said, just perfect. So perfect, the next day she crept out of the hospital, not even stopping one last time to look at her baby. She knew she could never give her child what she deserved, and hoped by leaving the child, she was giving her a half decent shot at life.

"She would've been your age and sometimes when I look at you, I think ... Look," she said, getting down on her knees and pulling out a baby basket from under her bed, "here are all her things."

There was a bow over the basket that must have been bright once, but was now faded with age, and the cellophane covering the things in the basket was now cracked and opaque. Inside the basket were little chemises trimmed in pink and green, little baby booties, and once-white cotton nappies. How many times, I wondered, had she taken out these things and folded and refolded them, before putting them back into the basket. After she told me this, I loved Rachel even more than I'd ever loved her before.

Yes, I thought looking at my mother, she had made her choice and I had made mine. I could not desert Rachel.

When I went back to school, I was as ecstatic to see Annie as she was to see me. We hugged and touched and told each other, in detail, what had happened over our summer holidays. We were in the second form now, and Mrs. Jacobs, was our form teacher. She was less formal than Mrs. Clarke – though she also harped on about the school rules, always reminding us not to do *anything foolish* which could get us expelled.

One day, Mrs. Jacobs came into class with a mysterious look on her face, and announced that Annie and I should go to the principal's office. She did not say anything more, except that Sister Marie Claire wanted to see us immediately.

The classroom went very quiet, before erupting into whispers and stares.

"Go on girls," Mrs. Jacobs continued, ushering us out of the class, "off to Sister Marie Claire."

I began searching my mind to see if I'd done anything wrong, but I could think of nothing. Annie also had a very puzzled look on her face. Our grades were still very high; in fact, we were still the two top students in our form.

Sister Marie Claire's office looked smaller on the inside than it really was, with paper everywhere. On the wall behind her desk were framed certificates from all the schools she'd attended abroad. From her window there was a clear view of the carrion tree near the cafeteria.

"Yes," Sister Marie Claire nodded, following my gaze. "It's a strange little tree isn't it. Not beautiful in the usual way, but in its own way. Now, what I really want to talk to you girls about is the excellent work you've both been doing here at All Saints. Really good work. From first form until now. We're developing a new programme here, a programme started by the old girl's association focused on getting more of our girls into universities and colleges, here in Jamaica or abroad. It will be a lot of work over the next few years," she warned, "but I think both of you girls are up to the challenge, yes?"

Up to such a challenge! What was Sister Marie Claire talking about? I was more than up to such a challenge! Good God! Wait till I got home and told Mama and Rachel! When they heard the news they would both be so happy for me! Already I could see myself going off to college and becoming the doctor my mother and grandmother always said I should become!

"Can you imagine!" Annie was saying excitedly when we were outside the principal's office, "the two of us! College together! We'll have to go to the L'Université de Laval in Quebec! That's where my parents met and where my sisters are going to school! Can you believe it?"

"I can hardly believe it!" I replied, hugging her back. I could hardly wait for school to be over so I could rush home and share my good news.

But my news was eclipsed. Mama and Zekie had done much better than either of them had expected and, instead of finding a house in Constant Spring, as they'd hoped, they landed one in the hills overlooking Kingston. Of course, their house wasn't as large as some of the other houses around – it did not have the guest cottages in the back, for one thing – but it was right where Mama always wanted to live, among the people with whom she'd always felt she should live. A house, Mama kept chanting, a house in the hills, the most bedazzled look on her face. And they'd gotten the house at a good price too, for the family living there was fleeing the island because of the rising crime and murder rate, and were willing to sell to the first person who could pay them cash up front. Zekie, I heard, had handed them a suitcase full of money. When I heard this a lump formed in my throat, but I said nothing. Could say nothing. Especially now when my mother was so happy. Still I wondered what the owners of the house must have thought, and was relieved I was not there to see their faces – a man handing them a suitcase full of money.

The house! When I was taken there a few days later, I could not believe it was ours. Large and airy, with floor to ceiling glass doors which opened onto a patio with a well-manicured lawn. Fir trees lined the driveway up to the house, and there was an orange grove at the back with many ripening fruits. There was also a small maid's quarters inside the house, but Mama insisted she wouldn't have a helper, she would clean her own house – now she had a house worth cleaning.

"I'll clean it from top to bottom! Make sure everything is in its place! Can someone pinch me so I know this is really happening!" She was already trying to figure out where she would put everything, and what colours to repaint the house. After a while she took Zekie's hands in hers, and the two of them just stood there, in the sunset, looking at the huge white house.

While they waited to finalize the sale, Mama forbade me to breath a word about the house to anyone in the yard. "Not even Rachel."

"Mama!" I protested, but she raised her hand to me.

"Not even Rachel," she repeated, and I could tell that she was serious. She didn't want people getting into her business any more than they already were. Now, if she took a day off work, the people in the yard dropped comments, now that she was a millionaire, she didn't need to go to work any more. It didn't seem to matter to the yard people where the money came from; all they wished was they were the ones who had it.

"A millionaire?" Mama laughed incredulously at Miss Sarah one day, who was teasing her at the standpipe. "I wouldn't even know what a million dollars look like!"

"Well…if *you* don't know what a million dollars look like, then your gentleman–friend certainly does."

Mama smiled, but she did not answer.

A few weeks later, Mama and Zekie got married in a simple ceremony before a Justice of the Peace. Grandy was there, finally meeting the man she'd heard so much about. Grandy looked Zekie up and down for a long time, taking him in, trying to make sense of him. I could see her mind working overtime: the flashy clothes, all that jewellery. Zekie knew what Grandy was doing, but pretended he was perfectly comfortable with having her eyes on him. For the week before the wedding, she watched his every move, trying to weigh him up and his intentions towards her daughter. Hushed quarrels followed between her and Mama when Zekie was not there. Finally, two days before the wedding, she said to me, "I just hope your mother knows what she's doing."

After the wedding, I felt even worse about keeping Rachel in the dark. "Mama," I pleaded, "let's tell Rachel something. Anything. Let's tell her you got married; that we'll be moving."

"If you do such a thing I won't be responsible for my actions!" she answered through her teeth. "Don't go broadcasting my business all over the place! People are bad-minded and don't like to see other people prosper! I don't want what happen to my father to happen to Zekie! I don't want to wake up one morning and find him gone!"

Some nights my mother would jump out of her sleep, searching the bed, making sure that Zekie was still there beside her. I knew she feared that one day she would wake up and it would all have turned to dust. "Don't mention a word to anyone!" she warned me. "Anyone!"

As it was, I felt the people in the yard knew what was going on, but they just chose not to say anything. Mama increasingly kept away from them. As far as she was concerned she'd already moved out and wanted to put the yard and its inhabitants far behind her. In her mind, she was already living on the hills.

Despite Mama's threats, as indirectly as I could, I started dropping all sorts of hints to Rachel. I did not want the day to come without her knowing about it. In breaks between the endless packing, I would slip out of the house and over to her room. She'd developed a sore on her leg, which would not heal and kept oozing pus. Her room now always smelled of medication, and was collecting a thick layer of dust. She was back to staying home and could not go to the wharf. The doctor said her body had gotten used to the first medication, and he would have to find some new medication to put her on.

Every morning before I left for school and every evening as soon as I came home I went to see if there was anything she needed. I opened the windows to let fresh air in and tidied up as best I could. I made breakfast for her, made sure her pitcher was full of clean water, and that she always had something to eat. She'd lost so much weight she seemed a ghost of her former self.

"What would I do without you?" she often asked, and I was beginning to wonder about this myself.

"Rachel," I said, a little before the move, "I have something to tell you."

"What is it, my pet?" she asked, rising up from the bed with her last ounce of strength, "You not pregnant or anything?"

"Oh no, nothing like that!" I quickly replied, indignant she could even think such a thing. There were one or two boys from our brother school, St. Stephens, I admired, but nothing had developed beyond an initial crush.

"Then what is it?" She fell back onto the bed, relief on her face.

I did not know where to begin. "Rachel, don't you have any family at all to come and help you out?"

"Why?" she asked, suspicious. She'd always said all her family were dead, that she was the last of her tribe. "Am I becoming a bother to you, Gloria? For if I am, you can just tell me."

"Rachel, you know you could never be a bother to me. I love doing things for you. But suppose I wasn't here to take care of you, then what would you do?"

"I can take care of myself!" she said, but the cough that wracked her frame shortly after was enough to say this was not the case.

"Anyway, why you asking me all these questions, Gloria? Something going on I should know about?"

"I might not be around much longer," I answered softly.

She was quiet for a long time, processing this information. "How much longer?"

"Very soon."

"Days or weeks?"

"Days."

She looked as if she had received a terrible blow. "I didn't think Zekie would come back to Jamaica to live in this yard, if he had any choice over the matter, but at least your mother could've said something. I don't grudge her... I would get out of this yard too if I could, still she could've said something..."

She sounded so lost I wanted to weep. "Don't you have *any* family at all, Rachel?"

She thought about this for a while, before saying. "Did anyone ever hear from Nilda?"

"No," I said, shaking my head. "No one never did."

Nadia still went to the police station, but there was no word about Nilda. The police were not taking the case too seriously because, as they put it, it was not as if Nilda had been abducted. She had gone willingly with the man, even if she was underage. She knew what she was getting herself into, but they would be keeping the case open just in case something did turn up.

"That girl should've come and talked to me before running away. I would've known what to tell her."

A lump formed in my throat that started spreading.

"I bet that man promised the poor foolish girl all sorts of things. I bet he told her how much easier her life would be with him. I bet she really wants to come back home but is too ashamed to do so. I bet she thinks about her family night and day, wondering how they doing. She miss her family terribly, but she don't know how to come back home again. When you leave like that you can't never come back home again. I wish that girl would've come to talk to me. I would've known what to tell her. All the consequences. Promise me one thing, Gloria." Rachel said, reaching up to grasp my hand tightly. "You will never be that foolish. You will never let some man turn you around! You will never leave like that. Promise me that, Gloria."

"I'll try." I said, tears gathering in the corners of my eyes.

No one was surprised the day we were leaving, and Mama was more than a little ashamed when, after all the things were packed into the vans, she took hold of my hand and said I should accompany her around the yard to say our goodbyes. Her first stop was at Rachel's. She hesitated outside Rachel's door for such a long time that, for a moment, I thought she would not go in, but she finally mounted the steps. Rachel was in bed and the room was dark because all the windows were closed and the curtains drawn. She kept insisting she did not want anyone to see her in this condition. She was literally wasting away.

"Rachel," Mama said, pausing for a long time in the darkened room and listening to Rachel's laboured breathing, "I am leaving."

Rachel could have made Mama uncomfortable by asking,

"Leaving where?" and pretending she did not know what Mama was talking about, but she did not. Instead, she fixed Mama with a blank stare, then looked away from her to the closed window.

Mama shifted uneasily. "Rachel, look, I feel bad enough about this. I probably should've said something before, but you know how it is."

Rachel looked past Mama to me.

"Come Gloria, give me a kiss."

"No!" Mama said, holding onto me, preventing me from going over. Lately she had outright forbidden me to see Rachel, insisting that whatever Rachel had might be contagious and she didn't want me catching it. I was to stay as far away as I could from her.

Rachel looked pained and very tired. Finally she said, "Come see me when you get a chance, Gloria. Close the door on the way out."

I pulled away from Mama and made my way over to Rachel. I sat down on her bed and took her fingers in mine.

She was crying, and before long I was crying too.

Mama stood where she was for a long time, looking at both of us. God only knows what was going on inside her. So many different emotions crossed her face. She was resolute, then sorry, then close to tears, then resolute once more. She was beginning to understand that whether or not she talked to Rachel, she would always care about her, that Rachel had long claimed a part of her heart and was not letting go. After a while she took a deep breath: "Gloria, it is time to go. Rachel, I'll be in touch."

Outside, Mama acted as if nothing had happened in the room, but I could see she was having difficulty controlling her emotions. After she regained her composure, Mama started moving through the yard. Our next stop was at Miss Sarah.

When Mama called her, Miss Sarah came out of her room and held onto me tightly. Her fingers were old, gnarled and as wrinkled as ginger-roots. Her hair was all silver. Lately, after a bad fall, she was using a cane.

"So you off now, my dears." Just the look in her eyes told me how much I pleased her. How much I'd always pleased her. She didn't wait for an answer, but continued, "I sorry you didn't get

to meet my girl. She promise me faithfully she coming this year."
She gave a toothless grin. "And you must all keep in touch."

"We will," Mama answered for both of us.

"You sure?" Miss Sarah cocked her head to the side, studying
Mama. She seemed to know more about my mother's motives
than my mother was prepared to admit.

"Look, I have to go." Mama was getting impatient. "I leave
some things in the house for you, some curtains and pots and
things; make sure to get them. Some of the things are for Nadia;
make sure she gets her things too."

"I will, I will," Miss Sarah said softly. "Thank you. And I truly
wish the best for you all. Especially you, Gloria. Come see us
again soon."

From Miss Sarah we went to see Miss Christie. Mama knocked
hard on the door and Denise had just enough time to open the
door before she had to take off after her son, Kevin, who was
scampering naked about the house. It was hard to believe this
child was now old enough to be running all over the place. He was
plump and brown. He hid behind the sofa, peering out every now
and again, squealing and taking off every time his mother made
after him. He seemed such a happy child, and seeing them
together brought a smile to my face.

"Ma!" Denise called out, "Gloria and Miss Rose here to see
you."

Miss Christie came through the multicoloured beads separating the living room from the kitchen, and tried to smile at us.
Though she tried to hide it, there was a look of pure envy on her
face. "So," she said, indicating Mama should sit down, "you
leaving."

Mama shook her head to the offer of a seat and said, "Yes, we
are leaving."

"Lucky for you. I can't lie – I wish it was me."

Kevin squealed and came running into the living room, making right for the centre table.

"Be careful he doesn't touch my furniture with his dirty
hands!" Miss Christie shouted to her daughter. Despite all the
years her furniture was still impeccable.

"Ma, his hands not dirty! I just bath him!"

"Well, I don't want his greasy fingers on my furniture!"

"Come, Kevin," Denise gathered her baby into her arms, "let's go outside." At the door she turned and said softly, "Bye Gloria."

"Goodbye," I replied, equally softly.

"Such a disappointment," Miss Christie said when Denise was out of the house. "Such a great big disappointment. Can you believe that girl pregnant again! For that no-good boyfriend of hers!" Miss Christie rolled her eyes up to the sky and shook her head.

"Well, the vans are waiting." Mama said. "Can't tarry too long here with you, much as I would like to!"

"Yes, you go along." Miss Christie seemed overwhelmed by everything. "Get Gloria out of this place as fast as you can. Like I say: I wish it were me!"

Our last stop was at Nadia's house. The younger children were outside and Nadia was washing some clothes and Nadine was helping her. Nadine was trying to put a white sheet on the line without it touching the ground, but she was too small and the line was too high above her and she was at it for a long time before she finally managed it.

I dreaded saying goodbye to Nadia. The few times she'd talked openly about Nilda's leaving, she always looked hard at me, as if she suspected I knew something, but was keeping my mouth shut. In truth, I wasn't sure why I was still keeping Nilda's secret, but keep it I did. Perhaps I wanted to believe, wherever she was, that Nilda had a better life than the one she'd had with her parents. Looking at the sad stoop that had crept up on Nadine, and how quiet she'd gotten lately, I wasn't sure that Nilda hadn't done the right thing. Still, the secret burned what felt like a hole deep inside my chest, and I'd taken to avoiding Nadia.

"Nadia," Mama called softly, to let her see that we were standing there, waiting to say good bye. Mama had always maintained a soft spot for Nadia.

Nadia looked up from her washing and gave us a small smile. "You finally finish packing?"

"Just now," Mama said.

Nadia's hands were pale and wrinkled from being in the water so long and she smelled of perspiration and bleach. She'd gone back to taking in washing so she could at least be home with the children.

"What can I tell you?" she said, "I wish it was me leaving this terrible, terrible yard, this terrible terrible place."

"Maybe one day." Mama continued softly. She treated Nadia as if she was a delicate figurine that could break at any moment.

"Oh, I don't know about that." Nadia was saying. "Not with the way things are going. Not with Jesus."

Mama looked away, unsure of what to say.

"And how I suppose to leave anyway? If I leave, how will Nilda find me? How will my little girl find me?" Her voice cracked, with bitterness, with a kind of disdain.

I looked away to the hibiscus tree I'd planted a few years before. Now that we were leaving, I'd wanted to uproot the tree and take it with us, because it was a sturdy plant that produced large bright red flowers. But Mama said this was silly and there was no guarantee the tree would grow in the soil at the new house.

"But soil is soil," I had insisted.

"No!" Mama shouted. "All soil is not the same soil and the sooner you learn that the better! That is why you're going to the school you're going to and that is why we are leaving this yard!"

I'd seen then a woman who would do just about anything to get me out of this yard, out of this life. A woman who wanted more, much much more for me than she'd had for herself.

"Here," Mama handed Nadia a piece of paper. "Here is my telephone number. Call me if you ever need anything. *Anything*. Or if you ever hear from Nilda."

Nadia looked down at the piece of paper for a long time. "I don't think I'll ever hear from that girl," she said finally and crumpled up the piece of paper.

After that, all I wanted to do was leave, to get as far away from the yard as possible. Perhaps I would do what Mama wanted me to do: forget about this place and forget about all these people I'd known and loved. Forget about the life I had lived here. But even as we walked away from Nadia, Nadine and the yard and headed for Zekie and the waiting vans I knew I was leaving a part of myself behind. Somehow I knew this would be the place that would never leave me, the place I would return to again and again, if only

133

in my dreams. This would be the place I would measure myself against, the place I would run away from and run back to. I began crying as Mama and I walked out of the yard into the vans and into our new life.

## CHAPTER 10

Looking back at it now, it seems that right from the start we did not feel as if we really belonged in the hills with its lawyers, doctors, and 'Indian' chiefs. These were people who carefully scrutinized any "suspicious characters" moving into "their" neighbourhood, and because of how quickly people were packing up and leaving the island it seemed there were always "suspicious characters" moving in. They felt they were losing ground to people like Mama, Zekie, and myself. What's more, they complained long and loud on the daily radio programmes. Some of these *characters* had more money than they did. Money made in all sorts of questionable ways in Canada, England, the United States. They developed ingenious ways of deciphering how long money had been *in-the-family* – and prided themselves on money being in *their* families from way back when – sugar canes and plantations. They formed committees to renovate the island's Great Houses, were on nightly television programmes talking about the need to restore the island's cultural heritage, fast falling into ruin; shouted loudly about *outsiders* like the Human Rights Commission coming in to tell us what to do with *our* criminals – *outsiders* who were forever talking about police brutality and an end to the death penalty.

When I was a little older, I began to recognise certain voices: "They ever lived a year in this place? On this island? *Our island*?" the wrinkled old men in beige linen suits asked each other, smoke from the tips of their Cuban cigars rising as pale, slender and elegant as their wives and daughters. "They know what manner of evil and mischief some of these people get up to? How they always want what they cannot have? How they want to take away what we have? Of course the police have a right to shoot and kill criminals! And, at the bottom of the hills, *they are all criminals!*"

The women saw themselves as the purveyors of decency. Saw themselves in a constant battle with the *loose types* at the bottom of the hill. Have you seen the clothes some of those women wear? The short shorts and tight pants? No decency. No decency at all!

Theirs were lives filled with the trials of getting good helpers who would not rob them blind. With these women, every move was carefully rehearsed and planned. You never saw two women meet on the street and, like Grandy and her friends, chat and laugh and touch each other. No family from the country ever showed up unannounced and stayed for weeks, getting in their way and becoming a general nuisance. They traded in colour, these women, and carefully tended to any bruise on their Sashas or Nicoles, for their daughters were to be blemish free.

At the time, for me the most disturbing thing about the hills was how quiet everything was. By nightfall the roads were deserted. During the day, the only people on the streets were helpers and gardeners and peddlers of all types; everyone in the hills had two, three or four cars. There wasn't the sound of children playing, or people quarrelling or fighting, or shouting their orders to shop keepers. In the hills, even the sound of the quiet was different. An altogether different place. An altogether different Jamaica.

Once we started living in the hills, Mama began dragging me with her on Sunday mornings to the old stone church at the bottom of the hill, where the hill women went. For the longest time no one paid any attention to us, but one day, a woman married to a Member of Parliament, a Mrs. Robatham, came over and introduced herself. "So," she said, all the while taking in my mother's clothes, her shoes, her watch, "I understand yours is the family that took over the Stockton place. Mary Robatham," the woman extended a gloved hand.

"Rose," Mama said, taking the woman's hand.

The woman waited for Mama to say her last name so she could begin running through the many branches of the interlocking family trees she somehow managed to keep stored in her mind, but Mama did not give her that chance, for she'd made that mistake once before.

"And who is the young miss?" the woman asked, turning her attention to me.

"Gloria," I replied.

"And what school is the young lady attending?"

"All Saints."

She brought her head forward as if she hadn't heard me correctly. "Did you say All Saints High School?" She smiled for the first time a genuine smile of recognition. "Well that's *my* old school too! Was that *your* school as well?" she asked my mother.

My mother nodded.

"Well," she was pleased with what she found, "we are all All Saints Girls here!" She thought about it for a moment, then added. "There is a women's group meeting this Wednesday here at the church. Why don't you come along, Rose? I think you will find that there are many All Saints Girls there!"

If Mama has any sense, *any sense at all*, I said to myself, she will get out of this as quickly as possible. In fact, if I were her, I'd stop coming to the church altogether. This was what Grandy kept telling her. "That ain't no proper church. No clapping and singing and turning around in that church! Nobody getting in the spirit! No place for you to be!"

At first, after we'd just moved into the great white colossus, Grandy had been awed, convinced a person could get lost in the house, telling everyone there were the acres of land around the house and sweet-sweet oranges growing in the back. But after a few days something began to bother her. It was the high white walls separating it from all the other houses around. Grandy concluded that whoever lived in the hills must be lonely in deed, for there was never anyone around to talk to. You couldn't just go to the fence and call to your neighbour to talk to them; you could barely see anyone passing outside on the road, the gate was so far away. In fact, Grandy complained, you could be dead for days without anyone knowing. She couldn't wait to get back to Lluidas Vale where though her no-good church sisters were always spying on her and taking her up to the pastor for all sorts of nonsense, at least there was always someone for her talk to, someone if she needed anything.

It should have been now, when my mother had achieved her

dreams – a house in the hills with a magnificent golden chandelier hanging from the high ceiling of the living room, and not a man but a *husband* – that everything should've fallen into place for her, but it did not. There was still the lingering feeling of something missing. We knew no one in the hills, and, when I was finally able to put my hands on it, I realized the hills lacked the vitality of the yard. Not that I wanted to go back to the daily fights, the long lines at the standpipe, the police incursions. All of that I was only too happy to live without. But somehow, despite all that went on in the yard, I felt safe there. I felt protected in ways I did not feel in the hills. People looked out for one another. Finally I started to see what Annie had been struggling with for years, and I was often reminded of her words when we first moved: "Now you will see. Now you will know." Yes, now I could see and now I did know Annie's sense of alienation and isolation. My mother felt even worse. She was often in the house by herself since she no longer worked; I at least got to go to school, and every morning Zekie literally ran out of the house back to where we used to live. He would spend the entire day there, lounging on the corner with his "boys", before he would creep home late at night to have the elaborate dinner Mama prepared. She often complained he only bathed and slept in the house.

Mama now complained of an ache inside her that was steadily growing worse, something slowly eating away at her. She'd gone from doctor to doctor taking numerous tests, but always the same result: nothing was physically wrong with her. Some mornings I would wake early to find her walking the grounds, touching this and that thing, looking about her. Yes, she had everything, but she behaved as if none of it belonged to her.

Now Mama had no problem with me visiting Annie, and she was pleased and relieved when Annie came to visit. I have to admit that the first time I went to Annie's house, I was astonished. Her family was even richer than I'd imagined. Gardeners, helpers, chauffeurs and cooks. Manicured lawn with so many different roses! Olympic-sized swimming pool, and the golden yellow poui tree in the back. Annie's bedroom was filled with stuffed animals of all kinds and framed pictures of her two sisters in Canada. They looked just like Annie, wild brick-red hair, freckles, hazel-green eyes. But they did not have the dare Annie always had in her eyes. A far more comfortable look on their faces.

I had been on the verge of telling Annie just how perfect her life seemed when I met her father. He looked me up and down as if I was something Annie had dragged in off the street. No wonder he and his daughter were always fighting. He was so very pompous, someone who was used to imposing his will on the people around him. I could tell his youngest daughter was forever exasperating him. Still, he held out a hand to me and welcomed me to his house. He had heard so much about me.

Annie's mother was totally different. She was forever fussing over Annie and me. She was a large handsome woman who wore long loose cotton caftan dresses and slippers about the house. She always had a handkerchief with her, because, despite years of living in Jamaica, a place she now called her "home", she'd never grown accustomed to the heat. She was the kind of person made for a large house, a staff, and three or four children. I liked her immediately, and I could tell she liked me too. The first time I went to visit, she took me outside to her garden. She had developed a bit of expertise on the island for roses, which came in the most fabulous of colours: oranges, fuchsias, various shades of violet and yellow. She'd even developed a rare saffron-coloured rose.

"When I first came to this island," she told me, bending over one of her flowers, examining it closely, "no one talked to me. Everyone was furious at Roy for bringing home a white woman. Child," she said, sounding very much like a Jamaican woman, "I had me the hardest time on this here island. Treated with such scorn! Such suspicion! Particularly by the home-grown whites," she said, winking at me. "I thought I would go crazy in the house by myself all day. I used to take Galaxy, my horse, and we would go riding in the hills. Sometimes we would be gone all day. All the time people kept shaking their heads and talking. Always watching me. I used to sketch in those days, nothing much, just the mountains, the sea, that kind of thing. One day I sketched a rose and from that moment I was hooked. I started drawing and then painting more and more roses, until that wasn't enough. I had to have the real thing. These flowers here," she said, pointing to her roses, "they were my solace when Roy was out to work and the children were off at school.

Since I had no one to talk to during the day, I poured all my energies into these flowers."

She leant back and looked at me. She was wearing a broad straw hat to keep off the sun. "And just you look at that. Now I don't have hands enough to handle all the orders I get for my flowers. Now," she said, smiling, as if to say she had gotten her just rewards, "both me and my flowers are accepted most everywhere we go – we are both naturalized Jamaicans." She was delighted that Annie-the-difficult, as she called her daughter, had a friend and I knew this little talk was her way of thanking me for being her daughter's friend. Later that evening, when I was going home, she presented me with several cuttings of her prizewinning roses.

Every few weeks I went to visit Rachel. Again she seemed better, even though she hadn't regained the weight she'd lost. She was seeing a new doctor who was giving her medication that was helping. The only drawback was the doctor had told her she'd have to keep taking the medication and go to the clinic for weekly checkups. She kept insisting she never felt better. "So", Rachel said, patting her bed for me to sit down, "tell me all about your new house."

I hesitated. I did not feel right telling her how big the house was, so big it was possible for Mama and I not to see each other for days if we didn't want to. I did not feel right telling her that I enjoyed walking the grounds, had even started a little garden of my own with the cuttings Annie's mother had given me.

"Go on," Rachel prompted, seeing my hesitation, "tell me. I can take it."

"Well, it is real quiet up there. And big."

"And you have your own room?"

"Yes! I have my own room!"

"You must be happy about that."

"Very happy."

She took a deep breath. "And your mother? How she doing?"

"Doing well. She said to tell you hello."

Rachel grunted as if she did not believe me.

I was not lying. While Mama never came out and asked me how *Rachel* was doing, she always asked me how "my friend" was doing, when she knew I had visited. She always said this with a wry twist, as if she was trying to make a joke of asking, but it never sounded like a joke.

"And you, how are you doing?" I asked her.

"As well as I can, I suppose. Good thing I've been putting a little money away; this medication eating me out of house and home."

"And who is helping you with the cleaning now?" I asked, looking around the room, which was spotless.

"I pay someone to come in once a week. She not you ..." Rachel smiled ruefully, "but she will do."

When I visited Rachel I often looked up the other women in the yard. It was more difficult to visit some women than others, but I usually made all the stops. One stop that was especially difficult was Miss Christie. "Yes," Miss Christie said, when she saw me looking at Denise' very plump body, "I just wonder where she going put this one, when she hardly have place to put herself and the one she has already!" She shouted this loud enough for Denise to hear. Denise did not answer. She was in the bedroom taking care of her child. She had come out briefly to say hello, not looking the least bit embarrassed about being pregnant again; indeed, she had a sweet almost serene look in her eyes and a glow to her face. Now she would have two children to love, her eyes seemed to say. Two children to take care of. Her children's father, I'd heard, now had a job at the post office and did his best to support Denise and the children, although he still lived in his mother's house.

"Such a disappointment! Such a blasted disappointment!" Miss Christie exploded. "You want something to drink?"

"No, no." I shook my head. All I wanted to do was get out of that house.

She got up to stand next to the white lace curtains, surveying her house, the living room, the bedroom, the closed door of the bathroom. She seemed for a moment to be surveying her life. She looked at me with such malice in her eyes, I got up quickly and told her it was time to leave; my mother would be wondering where I was, and I still had Miss Sarah and Nadia to visit.

"Tell me," she clutched my arm preventing me from leaving, "what is it like living up there?" She used her chin to indicate the dark blue mountains rising in the distance.

I did not know where to begin; I did not want to get into this kind of discussion with her.

"You don't need to answer me," she said, letting go of my arm. "I know what it is like. Had that life in the palm of my hand once, and then I let it go, just like that!" She snapped her fingers. "Yes, go on," she said, when she saw me edging towards the door. "Go back to your big white house in the hills!"

Outside, when I looked back, I saw her looking at me from behind the lace curtains. She seemed a shadow woman, a hidden woman, a woman who'd never got what she wanted. She reminded me of so many of the women I knew.

Miss Sarah was now confined to her room because she was virtually blind, but she knew who I was immediately when I walked into the room and her face brightened. Like Rachel, she now had someone coming in and helping her out in the house. "Well, just look at you!" she squinted the better to see me. "So grownup! Now, you're almost a woman! Come closer, come closer my dear, so I can get a good look at you. How old are you now?"

"Fifteen."

"And what year are you in school now?"

"Third form."

"Soon time for your examinations."

"And your daughter?" I asked, coming and sitting down beside her and taking her hands into mine, "Is she coming to visit this year?"

"It didn't work out for last year, but she promised me faithfully she coming this year!"

It was all so sad. I knew her daughter would never come, but I also knew Miss Sarah had to continue believing that she would, because to recognise the alternative was too painful. "Well, when she gets here, you have to let me know so I can come and meet her."

"I will, I will." She patted my hands gently. "You such a good child. Such a good-good child."

I knew I should stop and say hello to Nadia, but I did not. I was afraid of the unanswered questions always in her eyes. I did get a glimpse of Nadine, however, perched on the stoop of the steps, her head hanging. She could have been a replica of Nilda.

# PART TWO

# CHAPTER 11

Now that I was eighteen, Grandy would sometimes joke with me and tell me that love was like a river after a hard shower of rain, that if someone was not careful, love could overflow its banks. "You not to *fall* in love," she would tease, "you should *stand* up in it. For if you not careful, if you *fall* in love, love will wash you away. It can make you do all sorts of foolish things you might later regret." Now I was in love. And I wasn't standing up, or carefully wading out into the waters, as Grandy had told me to do; I had fallen in headfirst, was swept away in love's strong and heady currents. If I was a piglet and love was my mud, then I guess you could say I was wallowing in it. His name was Rafael and I looked up one Saturday at the library and there he was, studying. Tall, lanky boy with honey-coloured eyes and tight dark curls. He must have known I was staring at him, because he looked over at me and smiled and I quickly looked away.

Annie, observing this, rolled her eyes. No boy ever caught *her* fancy, although she'd caught the fancy of many a boy. She routinely found them foolish and did not suffer them gladly. That afternoon, shortly before the library closed, one of Rafael's friends came over and asked for my telephone number.

"Don't send it!" Annie whispered, and I looked at her as if she was crazy. Who was she to tell me what to do? There were enough people in my life doing this without Annie joining them. At that moment it was as if I was looking at her for the first time and from a great distance. She was a tiny stick figure whose mouth was moving, saying something, but not anything I wanted to hear. I quickly scribbled down my telephone number and sent it.

"Just remember," Annie said, annoyed, "we have exams to study for."

Exams, exams, that's all we ever talked about. Ever since the day Sister Marie Claire called us into her office and told us the "good news" about being in the "pilot programme", we'd started preparing for exams. Now it was our last year of school and we went from one extra lesson class to another. As part of the programme, Sister Marie Claire had recruiters come in and speak to the six of us who were involved in it. One day, while attending one of the presentations, I picked up a catalogue about studying in America. The name of one place jumped out at me: Minnesota. It seemed cold and distant, intriguing. A place I'd never heard anyone from Jamaica going to. Why did it suddenly seem to me that this was the exact place where I most wanted to go?

Annie, seeing me with this catalogue, gave me a puzzled look. "Oh no," she said, playfully wagging a finger at me, "we have decided that we're going to Canada *together*. Don't even start thinking about America!"

She had both our lives so carefully planned out. We were both going to study in Canada. L'Université de Laval. Why had I allowed her to do this? Now everyone, it seemed, was convinced that this was the best thing to do – go to school in Canada. All but my mother. She wanted me to stay right-here-in-Jamaica-where-I-can-at-least-keep-my-eyes-on-you!

Sad, lonely, Mama. Over the years she'd made one or two friends in the hills, but nothing approaching the intensity of the friendship she'd had with Rachel. She still attended the Wednesday evening church group, and went to the service at the bottom of the hill most Sundays, but not once had her home been selected to host a cocktail party. Not once had any of her "friends" dropped by to visit her. Not once was she featured in the *Sunday Gleaner*. The rumour was that her husband was one of those who had gotten-rich-quick in New York. As such, his money was less valuable. One day, when the pressure got to her, Mama shouted, "At least he did not make his money on the backs of black people!" Years later I realized this was how she justified – how we both justified – taking Zekie's money. And-who-knows-how-these-people-made-*their*-money-in-the-first-place? Oftentimes I saw her looking around as if reaching for something she'd had a long time ago, for someone whose name she now refused to call.

Once, I suggested she accompany me on one of my visits to Rachel, but she shrugged and declined. She'd made such an unnecessary mess of everything, she said, she could never face Rachel again. She was pleased with me though, she kept saying, glad I'd kept my head held high, and hadn't done "anything foolish" to get-myself-in-trouble.

Rafael phoned that evening and we talked for hours. After that, we talked almost every night for hours. It was like it had been with Annie all over again.

"A distraction," Annie kept saying, "that boy, what's his name again? Yes, Rafael, he's nothing but a distraction, and you have your school work to focus on."

She'd taken an instant and total dislike to Rafael, though she couched her dislike in terms of Rafael being a "distraction." Now she was always telling me to focus on my schoolwork; sometimes I had to wonder if this was the same girl whose parents had to drag to school that first morning. I was beginning to feel that Annie's embrace was a little too tight, our friendship a little too close; it was developing the overpowering scent of the fleshy white cereus which bloomed only at night. When I was younger, this closeness was welcome, for my only wish then was to be lost in Annie and for Annie to lose herself in me, to have the gaping emptiness and numbness I had been carrying around inside me filled. This was no longer the case. I was beginning to feel that Annie and I were two separate and distinct persons.

Once Rafael entered my life, my friendship with Annie started to unknot. It wasn't that it collapsed all at once; no, it happened over the weeks and months. Now I wanted to spend more and more time with him and less and less time with Annie. When I went to the library on Saturdays, I went specifically to see Rafael. When Annie realized this she was furious.

"That boy!" she would say through her teeth, "He'll be the cause of your undoing! If you don't get to college, you'll have him to thank!"

One Saturday Rafael took me to the back of the library, leaned me against the rough wall and put his large pink tongue between my lips and kept moving it in and out and in and out of my mouth. At first I did not know what to do with myself, how to feel about what Rafael was doing to me, but after a while I started to relax, to close my eyes and enjoy what he was doing. I was breathless when we finished and could barely look at him.

"There's nothing to feel ashamed about," Rafael said. "I only have the best intentions towards you."

I did not know what to think. This went against all the things I had been told about boys and men – by Grandy, by Mama, by the nuns and teachers at school. Boys were dangerous. They could blighted one's future. But here was Rafael telling me he had only the best intentions towards me. I was well and truly confused.

Rafael must have guessed what was going on in my head because he said, "Gloria, I will never force you to do anything that you don't want to do. I have been watching you for months, trying to get up the courage to talk to you. I would never do anything to hurt you. I will never force you to do anything against your will."

After that, I started lying to Annie, finding all sorts of excuses why I couldn't meet her at the library on Saturdays. She was furious! She knew, without me telling her, that I had started to spend my Saturdays with Rafael instead. At first she pretended she could take all this in her stride, but when Saturday after Saturday I could not see her, she grew more and more upset. If I had looked closely at her, I would have realized that something in her was unravelling. But as far as I was concerned, the few hours I got to see Rafael on Saturdays was the only time I could be with him all week. I could not take him to my house to meet my mother (she who knew nothing of his existence); and I didn't feel ready to go to his house. I was more than happy for Annie to join Rafael and I some of the times we went out, but the few times we did this had been a total disaster. Annie barely said a word to Rafael, and when Rafael decided to bring one of his friends to keep Annie company, Annie was even more stand-offish to the friend than she was to Rafael. As far as I was concerned, it was her fault that we did not see each other any more on Saturdays. It was all her fault, I convinced myself, as I told her yet another lie as to why I could not meet her at the library on Saturday.

At the same time I was lying to Mama, telling her I had to go to the library every Saturday, that Annie and I needed this time to study because our final exams were fast approaching.

Mama began wondering aloud why I seemed so happy to be rushing to the library to "study". Why I was always dressing up just-to-go-and-study. As if, she said, studying and going to the library had become the most pleasant things in the world to do.

I did not care. I lived for the times when I could see Rafael. One Saturday we went to the botanical gardens. Crawled under the weeping divi-livi tree sweeping the ground. Rafael gently removed my shirt, then my bra, and stared and stared at my full round breasts. He then took them into his hands, my breasts, his fingers passing ever so lightly over my nipples sending the most exquisite sensation through my body. He bent close and brought his lips to my breasts and started kissing, then biting them. My fingers and toes curled of their own free will. He then started kissing me all over, both of us groaning. I could not believe all these feelings had been buried deep inside my own body. It was as if, all along, a beast had lain hidden inside me, some animal that was now awakening. I wanted Rafael to keep touching and biting me forever. When we were finished there were many tiny purple marks all over my neck, shoulder and breasts.

"I love you," he said, circling one of the purple marks.

"I love you too," I replied, snuggling close to him.

"How are classes coming along?" he wanted to know.

"Fine," I replied. "We've been studying very hard, Annie and I."

"Annie." He chuckled at her name. "She doesn't like me very much does she?"

I did not answer him.

"Oh, you don't have to say anything. I *know* she doesn't like me."

"But I like you," I said, trying to get even closer to him. "And that's all that matters. How is *your* studying coming along?" We were both preparing for the same exams.

"They're coming. They're coming."

149

"Which schools are you applying to?" I asked, thinking he must be applying to colleges in Canada, England and the United States. After all, wasn't this everybody's dream? He raised up on his elbow, and looked down at me, slightly puzzled. "I'm only applying to one university," he said, "the one here in Jamaica. And you?"

I started stumbling over myself. "The nuns at school ... they told me I should apply to as many as I can... I'm applying to schools in America ... Canada ..."

"Why?" he asked, totally baffled.

Again I started stumbling over myself. "The nuns ... Annie is going to college in Canada ... if I get into a school in Canada ... Or even here in Jamaica, I will stay."

He lay back down, his hands behind his head. "I don't see why I should go some place else to study what I can study right here in Jamaica. I want you in my life, Gloria. Really, I do. Think about going to school here in Jamaica."

And what would I tell Annie? And the nuns at school who'd worked so hard for me, filling out application forms, paying application fees, applying for ever more scholarships? What would I tell all these people? A dense grey cloud started settling over my mind. Out of the cloud Annie arose, pointing an accusing finger. She'd known me long before I met Rafael, and we'd both set our sights on going to college together in Canada. Long-long before he'd entered the picture. How could I do this to her, she was screaming in my mind. A huge lump of guilt formed in my throat. And Grandy, what would I tell her? She said she would miss me if I went away, "but think of the opportunity, Gloria. This once-in-a-lifetime opportunity. You cannot let this opportunity pass you by."

I looked at Rafael. God, he was handsome! The most handsome man in the world. And smart. And going to be an engineer. Already I had started placing his last name next to mine, just to see how it would look. The more I did this, the more right it seemed. These days I felt more comfortable with him than with anyone else. I wanted to give myself to him. To have him totally possess me. I was sure this was the man I would marry. I nuzzled up closer to him and put his arms around me.

That evening when I got home, Mama was sitting in the dark in the living room and it seemed she had been sitting there waiting for me.

"Where have you been, Gloria?" Mama asked as soon as I turned on the lights.

"At the library," I answered easily.

"Gloria, I'm asking you again. Where have you been all day?"

From the tone of her voice I knew something was wrong. She got up from the sofa where she had been sitting and walked over to me. She'd been sitting there for hours, it seemed, watching the clock and waiting for me.

"I told you," I answered edgily, looking at her out of the corners of my eyes, watching to see what she was doing, "I was at the library."

She brought out a thick brown belt from behind her. "Liar! Damn disgusting liar! Annie called here, looking for you, said you told her you weren't feeling too well, weren't sure if you'd be going to the library. So I took the car, went looking for you there. Stupid me, thinking you might really be sick. There wasn't a sign of you. So I'm asking you again, Gloria, where have you been all day?"

She was coming towards me with the belt and I did not know what to do. Mama had never beaten me before. For all the times she and I had quarrelled, she'd never raised a belt to me. What was I going to do? Zekie, as usual, was not in the house. Mama and I were totally alone. I'd never seen her this angry in all my life. There was so much anger and hurt in her eyes.

"All right," I said, realizing I was cornered, "First I went to the library, then I went to the botanical gardens with a friend."

"And which *friend* is this?" she asked, eyeing me up and down, disdainfully. "Anybody I know?"

I didn't like the tone of her voice, the look in her eyes. I started backing away from her, but she grabbed me by the front of my blouse. The grasp was so hard some of the buttons came off in her hand and my blouse opened, showing the small purple marks all over my neck and chest.

"Well, well, well," she said, standing back and looking at me. "What do we have here? What are these, Gloria?"

151

I did not answer her and was now really panicking. I could see from the look on her face she thought she understood only too well what I'd been up to. Her face said more than the purple love marks had happened.

"So," she brought up the belt, getting ready to hit me, "I guess we have two women in this house after all. All along I was thinking it was just one! You children, you girl children, you just never learn, do you? You just don't listen, do you? I didn't learn when my mother tried talking to me, and now you're doing the exact same thing! Such a disappointment! Such a blasted disappointment!"

"Mama, don't do this!" I begged, struggling to get the belt from her. "Mama, please don't do this. Mama, please! Don't do this and I promise you, this will never happen again." She was now shaking and crying uncontrollably.

"Mama," I tried one more time, "this will never, ever happen again. Please."

She started twisting and pulling, trying to get the belt out of my hand. We were shoving things around the living room and grabbing at each other. She pulled off the rest of my blouse and now I was only in my bra. She stopped and looked at the marks all over my chest, shaking her head from side to side in angry disbelief.

"Look what I have happening in my own house! Look at this child's neck and shoulders and breasts! All the time I'm here trying to raise you decent! Believing you decent! You belong in that yard! You belong with those people! Just look at you!"

"Decent? You call this place and all these people decent? Mama they talk about you behind your back! They laugh at you! They laugh at us! As for Zekie, he is the laughing stock of these hills! You ever see anyone coming to our house? How come no one ever comes to visit? How about that women's group you belong to? Decent?"

This enraged Mama even more. Lately, she'd started bothering Zekie, telling him we needed to move into an even bigger house, one with guest cottages in the back. Perhaps then people would come to visit. Perhaps then she would get her house in the newspaper. Every day she was on to him about this, as she'd been on to him about moving out of the yard.

"You think moving into a bigger house will solve our problems? Solve *your* problems, Mama?" I could not stop myself. "You think moving into a bigger, better place will make these people like us? Like *you*?" Tears were coursing down my face, my lips were trembling. I looked at my torn blouse on the floor, and the sight made me past caring.

"You should be ashamed of yourself!" Mama sobbed. "Fighting your own mother! You know what happen to children like you? Children who fight their own mothers? *Nothing good!* Nothing good can come of a child who fights her own mother!"

"I wasn't fighting you! You were the one fighting me!"

"I not raising *no* black birds to come in here and pick out *my* eyes! Don't you ever come into my house looking like that again! If you can't abide by my rules, then leave!" A terrible disgust came into her eyes as she looked at my half-clad body, her eyes lingering on my full breasts.

"Mama, you want me to leave and I want to go! I want nothing more in the world than to go! I want nothing more in the world than never to see your face again!"

"Ungrateful little wretch," she said under her breath.

## CHAPTER 12

Rachel was dead. Zekie came home with the news that she had been dead for two days before anyone found her body. How could this be? I had seen her just a few days before and she seemed fine. How could she be dead now?

"She died of AIDS," he whispered, as if there were people around who could hear him say the word. As if the word itself was dirty.

But the truth was that AIDS had become real on the island. Now there were people openly discussing it on the television and radio. Of course, most people kept saying that only "some people" got the disease, but every day there was a new story about some "decent person" who had contracted it. Men were told to use condoms. Even Rafael and his friends joked about always "having something on them." I looked at Rafael, who hastily looked away.

But Rachel? How could she be dead? The last time I saw her, she looked well enough. The medication the new doctor had given her seemed to be working.

"I need to be alone," I said, getting up to leave the living room where he and Mama were sitting. I felt as though I was stretched to the seams and coming apart.

For her part, Mama looked as if she could not believe what she was hearing. I realised then that she had always cherished the hope of one-day somehow making things up with Rachel. She had been missing her ever since she had come to the hills. Now there was no chance of making up. Mama looked as if she was doing everything she could to hold herself together. When she looked at me she had a long-lost look on her face and her eyes were blank. I could not bear to see that look, twin to all that was going on inside me. I turned from my mother and fled.

Inside my room my head kept spinning and spinning and spinning and I found myself on the floor. How could she die? I felt abandoned. I started desperately grabbing at all the images of Rachel I could find. There she was the day I passed my common entrance examination, coming to give me a big hug and an orange to eat; and before that, the times she cooked dinner for Mama and me; or when she stood up and fought off my father's wife for Mama. There she was the many times I quarrelled with my mother and sought refuge in her room. There she was when I came with my many questions, which she did her best to answer. She always had time for me, or always made time for me. It did not matter to her if my problems were big or small or medium-sized; she always listened. She was delighted when things went right for me, and helped me celebrate my accomplishments; she always provided a bosom to rest my head on when I needed to cry. It broke my heart to think of her dying alone in her room. Who had given her a shoulder to lean on when she needed it, the woman who had helped so many over the years? Who was there to hold her, to tell her everything would be all right? To let her know someone cared about her and loved her, that she had made a difference to their life?

I started emptying out my drawers, looking for a picture of Rachel. Had we ever had a photograph taken of us together? No, that had never happened. Somehow I knew, even then, that the only picture I would ever have of her would be the one of her in her coffin. How cruel for that to be my only picture of Rachel! A woman who had been so full of life! A picture of her in her coffin! Not one of her smiling, or laughing, or crying or cursing. Not even one when she was sick and holed up in her room! Not one picture of her when she was alive! But then, I had never seen Rachel with a picture of herself. None on the wall. None on the corner of her dresser. Why was this, I wanted to know, but it was too late to ask.

And her family? Were they still wondering about her, looking for her, as Nadia was still looking for Nilda? Were they still wondering about the girl, no more than thirteen years old, who had left home on the promises of a man? Did her mother, if she was still alive, still go down on her knees every night and wash the floor with tears and prayer, hoping the Lord would somehow bring her child home? Had they, long ago, given up on the possibility of ever finding Rachel, pretending she had never been born, or was long dead? Was Rachel even her real name, anyway? Her surname? Where exactly had she come from?

After the tears there came a resolution: I did not know where the money was coming from, but I was going to give Rachel a decent burial. I would go to the Kingston morgue to claim her body. I would find her a lovely dress, and have her hair nicely done up. Pay someone to put make-up on her face. I would buy her a burnished wood casket. I would pick out a spot in the cemetery, covered with green grass, because I wanted her to have a nice peaceful resting-place, after all the hardships of her life. I owed her that much. This was exactly what I was going to do.

More people came to Rachel's funeral than anyone could have expected. Everyone from the yard came and Miss Sarah and Miss Christie wailed so loudly that you would have thought it was their own sister who had died. Nadia came too, still with a cloak of despair around her shoulders. She looked up to the ceiling when Jesus stumbled in late. It seemed as if all the higglers, fishermen, streetwalkers and shop owners who worked around the wharf were there. There were even a few stray sailors at the funeral, sitting at the back of the room, shedding quiet tears. How the word had gotten out that Rachel had died and how so many people heard and found their way to the church, I still do not know. I only know that the place was packed. I watched as the people filed into the church in small groups. Rachel would have been pleased to see all the people who came. I don't think she realised how many lives she touched. The woman I claimed at the morgue, the twisted, emaciated figure, was not Rachel. Could never be Rachel. For me Rachel would always be the woman offering me a piece of fruit, listening to me when I needed to talk, hugging me when I needed a hug. The woman with the emerald green box. Looking down at Rachel in her coffin, it was hard to accept that I would never see her again, that I would not hear her raucous laughter again, that I would never hear her many gold bangles jingling again. The people in the yard told me that a few days before she died, Rachel started giving away everything – all her prized possessions. She'd flung her doors open and invited the whole yard in.

"Child," Miss Sarah told me, "it was something else to hear, how Rachel carried on, 'Come, take it all. The gold bangles, the bedspreads, the money. Come, take it all. What's the use? You can't take it with you when you go!' And she said how we should not hide away our best things hoping to make good use of them one day. 'Use them now!' she said. Then she threw out unopened duvet sheet sets, silk curtains, money and jewellery. She threw out everything but the furniture she had in her house."

For the last couple of days they'd been wondering about her, Miss Sara said. They'd heard her chanting and mumbling to herself in her room late into the night, bursting into a high wild laughter. They thought she was losing her mind.

Yes, I nodded, looking around the church at all the people gathered there, Rachel would have been pleased. Even Annie, who had never met her, was there. And Rafael. For a while I thought my mother would not come, but she slipped in as the service was about to begin and took a seat at the back of the church. Since the news of Rachel's death she'd been withdrawn, blank-eyed, refusing to eat. Zekie got so worried he stayed home with her. Once she looked up at me and said, "You know you have to be careful right? Don't touch the dead body or anything. People still have to be ever so careful about this disease."

I nodded my head yes.

Zekie was the one who had given me most of the money for Rachel's funeral. The rest I got from a collection in the yard. Two days before the actual funeral Mama came and dropped a stack of money in my lap, but walked away before I could say anything. I'd used all of this money for the nine-night ceremony and the funeral.

On Rachel's highly polished, purple-lined coffin were her favourite flowers, white Easter Lilies, my gift to her. In the coffin she wore a cream-coloured dress and a mock-gold crown. Even in death I wanted her to know she was a queen. Half way through the service Mama started crying uncontrollably, so badly that some of the women from the yard had to hold onto her and lead her out of the church. She was even worse at the cemetery. There she had held onto the coffin, trying to prevent it from going down into the ground. "I'm sorry Rachel," she kept saying, "I'm so very-very sorry."

She was inconsolable and the women again held onto her and lead her away from the graveside; Zekie then took her home.

After the funeral I went to Rachel's room. It was my private homage, something I had to do. The door swung open at my touch. Everything was in disarray. It was as if Rachel had spent the last moments of her life railing at all life had dealt her. The dishes were scattered on the floor and clothes, shoes, sheets, curtains – all the things Rachel so cherished in her life – were strewn about the room. I set to work.

I was almost at the end of my packing and cleaning when I found the emerald green box, wrapped up in a sheet in the far corner of the room. It seemed to be the one thing Rachel had taken care to protect. I held the box in my hands for a long time, and just holding something Rachel had held and cherished gave me a feeling of consolation. I opened the box and inside were all Rachel's letters. So many different letters, some from old suitors. Just what should I do with them? I gathered them up, thinking it was perhaps best to burn them, when I noticed several other pieces of paper at the bottom of the box. I reached for them and saw my name and Nilda's written on them. The writing was childish, awkward, as if done by someone just learning to write. I remembered the nights I quarrelled with Mama and came to Rachel's room to study. She would look at what I was doing, even though she pretended she was not looking. Part of her was always curious, seeking, convinced that with just a little education she could have had a far different life. I knew instinctively that she wanted me to have the box, had all along been waiting for the right day, the right moment to give it to me. The box was such a beautiful emerald green colour, so sturdy too with its own lock and key. I would keep Rachel's emerald green box. I would take good care of it for her.

## CHAPTER 13

I stopped lying to my mother about when I was going to see Rafael. I just got dressed and told her I was going out with "him" for the day. She would throw me a venomous look, but say nothing. I guess she hoped I had enough sense not to do anything to get myself in trouble. In any case, she was still dealing with her feelings over Rachel's death, and really did not have the energy to fight with me about Rafael. Since the day she came at me with the belt, we said as little as possible to each other. Like Annie, she'd taken an instant and total dislike to "him" when she finally met "him" at Rachel's funeral. But unlike Annie, I understood what her feelings were about. After all, when she was my age, a man had blighted her future.

Annie and I, good God, we were having so many difficulties! Barely talking to each other. Barely looking at each other. And when Annie could bring herself to look at me, there were such wounded, bitter looks! Rafael's was the only shoulder I had to lean on, and now, more than ever, I clung to him. Some Saturdays Rafael would borrow his mother's car and we would head out to the country. He was taking me all over the island, to places I'd never been before. He was intent, he said, on "selling" me on Jamaica. Then I would get the crazy idea out of my head about wanting to leave our country. Little did he know that I had pretty-much made up my mind to stay on the island. To stay with him.

How I loved this boy! Loved what his mother had done with him. When I first met her, she'd taken me into her arms, glad to meet the girl Rafael spoke so highly of. "So, I hear you're planning to leave us," she said to me one day, eyeing me playfully.

"I don't know about that," I'd answered, warily, for I was

constantly back and forth about what I was going to do with the rest of my life, never mind where I would study.

"Well I want to add my two cents to the discussion and ask you to stay. We need you here, to help build up our troubled, but wonderful country. America, Canada, England, they already have too many of our best talents. People who should be here building up Jamaica are giving all their energies to other countries. You should stay here!"

"But I would be coming back."

"Oh, that's what they all say! That's what Rafael's father said. He went away "to study" and never came back. Now he's married and living somewhere in New Jersey. Rafael, well, … he's different. He's not going anywhere. He's staying right here with me in Jamaica."

I did not like the way she talked about her son. As if he belonged to her, as if he was somehow beholden to her, but I said nothing. From what I could see this was how most mother's felt about their sons. But something started gnawing away at me. Oh, I could not exactly put my finger on it. Did not know if it was something to do with Rafael or his mother or them both. But there it was: A most uncomfortable feeling. There were times I tried talking to him, but you could tell he was only listening because he did not want to seem rude. And he had a way of looking at me – yes, as if he was simply being indulgent with me. Whenever we disagreed, he would simply state and restate his position, never changing it and I was the one who always had to change my mind or change my position. And then there was the way he talked about his mother, as if she were not his mother so much as a projection of perfect womanhood. Still, I comforted myself that day, it was flattering she liked me so much, Rafael's mother, that she wanted me, talked of me being in both their lives.

Rafael and I climbed the very cold, much-talked-about Dunn's River Falls, visited Yallahs Pond and Turtle Beach, rafted down the Rio Grande. We went to Nanny Town in the Blue Mountains and Rafael told me about Grandy Nanny, Maroon rebel leader who resisted the British. Of course I knew all this already but didn't disabuse him. I was beginning to realize that he liked to feel that he knew so much more than me. We went to the witch's house in Rosehall; and to Lover's Leap, the sheer 1600 foot drop from the Santa Cruz Mountains to the turquoise sea below. It was as if I was discovering the island for the first time. I told him about my summer holidays in Lluidas Vale, about Grandy and my friends there, about Uncle Silas, people I hadn't seen in years because I now spent my summer holidays working in Kingston. I told him especially about Junie, who had saved Yvette, and who seemed to know every plant on the island.

"*Every* plant, Gloria?" He smiled indulgently.

"That's how it seemed to me! I remember Junie always with a plant or some flower in her hand. I remember looking around her garden and asking her how she did it, how she kept so many different plants straight in her head. They all looked the same to me. She said to look closer, how all the leaves were different, how some leaves were a lighter green, others darker, and some an in-between green colour; how the sizes and the shapes of the leaves were all so different. Some broad and flat, others straight and slender, and some – I can still see her tracing her fingers around the curve of a cerasee vine – had a shape all of their own. She told me how easy it was to tell cerasee, the tiny pale yellow flowers on the vine and the small bright-orange fruits, and the seeds blood-red. She put the seeds into her mouth and started sucking on them. When I put the seeds in my mouth, I was amazed at how sweet they were, though cerasee tea, made from the leaves, is very, very bitter."

After telling Rafael – who barely seemed to be listening – this story I realized how much I was missing my grandmother, missing the country, missing my friends there. Grandy could no longer come to the city, her arthritis now so bad, and I'd been too busy to go to Lluidas Vale. But she still sent her letters – so many letters, which I'd kept, arranged in chronological order, in my room. Some were yellow with age, others crisp and new. Every now and again I took them up and read them for hours on end.

"Perhaps," Rafael said, talking one of my hands in his, "we should pay your grandmother a visit."

"Yes, that's something we should definitely do."

But even then I somehow did not believe him when he said we

would do this for we always ended up doing things Rafael wanted to do, or Rafael felt were things I should know or should have done already; rarely, if ever, did we do something – anything – I wanted to do.

I looked away to the mountains in the distance. The dark-blue mountains always in the distance. They had been such a constant in my life, these dark blue mountains. Everywhere we went on the island, they were there. I could not imagine waking up one day and not seeing them. How could I even think of going away and leaving all this? How could I even think of going away and leaving Rafael, even if only for a few years?

One Saturday, Rafael and I headed out to the country to meet an artist friend of his mother's. His mother had told him all about this man, a self-taught "intuitive" artist, who lived in the hills of Murray Mountains, in St. Ann. This man, Rafael told me, did the most amazing work, rolling mountains, voluminous white clouds in the sky, creating a truly mystical world. We headed for Ocho Rios, and from there took the road to Montego Bay, turning off and starting the steep ascent to Brown's Town, where we stopped at a restaurant to have lunch. Sitting there, looking out, I thought I saw a familiar face. At first I could not believe it. Was this the same face I hadn't seen in years? I got up from the table, and walked to the door of the restaurant to make sure. Yes, it was her! I was sure of it! It was that girl Yvette! Oh, but what a different Yvette, now a grown woman, tall and thin, wearing a bright yellow dress which was spectacular against her very dark skin. Her hair, which looked as though no chemicals had ever touched it, was plaited into a million tiny plaits. She was across the street, waiting for a bus or cab to take her down the hill to Montego Bay.

I couldn't describe all that started happening inside me. I felt that God had finally answered one of my prayers.

Yvette looked up from where she was standing and caught me staring at her. She flashed me an arrogant look, before her eyes started to melt in recognition.

"Gloria?" she mouthed softly. "Is that really you, Gloria?"

Immediately I was choked up. We started walking, then running towards each other. All the years I'd thought about this girl, dreamt about this girl! I'd come to believe I'd never see her again.

162

The world around us dissolved into a fuzzy backdrop of noise, heat, dust and colour. The only thing that was real, the only thing that made sense to me, was that Yvette was across the street and we were heading towards each other. We met in the middle of the road, started touching and touching each other. We held hands, as if to make sure that the other could not disappear again. I reached for her forehead, feeling for the mark I knew would be there. Thank God Brown's Town was a small place, with intermittent traffic, all the time we were in the middle of the road!

"I've thought about you," Yvette said, tears streaming down her face.

"I've thought about you too."

She started shaking her head from side to side, as if she still could not believe I was there in front of her. "Oh Gloria, if only you knew how much I've thought about you."

"I know, I know," I replied, lacing my fingers with hers. "Trust me I know."

She dragged me out of the road, back to the shade of the mango tree. Rafael came to the restaurant door and stood looking at us for a moment, before he shook his head and went back inside. Another-part-of-me-he-would-never-understand.

I wanted Yvette to tell me everything that had ever happened to her, to fill me in on all the years I'd missed.

"Oh, I've been here and there," she answered offhandedly. "This place and that … I leave for Grenada tomorrow. Yes," she said, answering the question on my face, "tomorrow."

I didn't know what to say. I'd just found her and here she was leaving me already. But this time I would not let her just walk out of my life, this time I would force my address into her hands and into her heart. No, she would not just up and disappear out of my life again. "And where again did you say you were going?"

"To Grenada."

"Grenada?" I had expected her to say New York, or Toronto, or even London. But not somewhere else in the Caribbean, and certainly not Grenada. Weren't there some political disturbances there recently? The president had been killed. U.S. soldiers had invaded.

"Why Grenada?" I asked, and it seemed she'd been asked that

question one time too many. I saw that the old Yvette, the one I'd known, and yes, loved, was still alive and kicking.

"What's wrong with Grenada? Why can't a body go there?"

For a moment we were the two girls at the river. Old adversaries. It was as if all those years had not passed, like sand, right through our fingers.

"I'm sorry. You're right, Grenada is somewhere to go just like anywhere else. I guess I'm just used to people going to New York, Toronto. How long will you be in Grenada?"

"Oh, I don't know," she said, as if she really didn't. "I'm moving there."

Yes, Yvette was still the same restless creature who'd spent the last few years moving from one place to another, never quite settling down, never feeling at home. Yvette, my dear friend Yvette.

I did not know how to put the next question, so I just blurted out, "Did you ever hear from you mother?"

Her face crumpled and she looked again like the sad little girl I remembered, the little girl who'd lost a mother, the little girl who was still looking for her mother. The girl who would always be looking for her mother. I was sorry I'd asked.

"No," she said after a while, "I never heard from my mother."

She did not need to tell me anything else, how she'd reluctantly come to the conclusion that perhaps her mother had died in America after all. How she'd lived with an aunt for a while, but could not get along with her and had moved from one aunt to another, from one cousin to another, from one place to another, never, not once, finding a place to settle down. She did not need to tell me she was now living with a man whom she was desperately trying to get away from, a man who had beaten her up time and time again, trying to control her, and this was why she was going to Grenada. She did not need to tell me any of these things, because somehow I knew, and she knew that I knew. That old connection was still so strong between us.

"I see the bus coming now and I have to get going," she said. "Come, write me your address quick-quick right here." She handed me a piece of paper and a pencil from her straw bag. I scribbled my address down as fast as I could. Then I held onto her, and she held onto me, until the bus came to a stop in front of us and she climbed in.

I watched as the bus began its slow descent down the hill to Montego Bay. Yvette pushed her hand through the window and kept waving a white handkerchief as the bus drove away. I watched until both the white handkerchief and the bus disappeared, hoping against hope that she would keep her promise and write to me when she got to Grenada.

## CHAPTER 14

Annie and I are sitting under the lignum vitae trees waiting our turn to go in for Sister Marie Claire's school-leaving interview. I am dreading this because I will have to admit to Sister Marie Claire that I've decided to stay in Jamaica. What will Sister Marie Claire think of this? Then there would be my grandmother and Zekie to tell – and my mother. Not to mention the young woman sitting beside me. My stomach is in knots; I cannot stop fidgeting. All the time Annie kept watching me, as if she knew something was up with me, but we rarely traded confidences any more. In anticipation of the interview I'd kept practising, trying to get the right words out, said them in front of the bathroom mirror at home, even practised with Rafael and his much too delighted mother.

Annie and I were so estranged now, that I could not figure out why we still clung to each other. Such intense feelings of resentment and anger. We still sat in class together, ate lunch together, and if you'd asked anyone they would have told you we were still the best of friends. Not once did we speak about Rafael, whom, I knew, Annie wished would just disappear in the wind. But she was biding her time because she still thought we would be going to Canada together. Oh what a Judas I was! Oh what a betrayer!

Even though I dreaded it, it was a relief when my name was finally called. I hurried away from Annie's suspicious eyes. But as soon as I was in Sister Marie Claire's office, as soon as I was ensconced in a chair, tears started pouring from my eyes. I was confused. I was afraid. I really didn't know what I was going to do. Sister Marie Claire must have been used to scenes like this because she just sat there for the longest time and allowed me to cry. When I'd gotten hold of myself, she led me over to two seats by the window with a perfect view of the ancient and gnarled carrion tree.

"You see that tree," she said, holding my hand and smiling, "that tree is our tree. You know that, right?"

I nodded. I had come to love what so many at the school called the ugly old tree.

"Do you want to know my story about that tree, Gloria? Do you want to know why it matters so much to me?"

I nodded.

"Well, this year All Saints will be twenty-five years old. Twenty-five years! It's so hard for me to believe this! This school has taken up twenty-five of the best years of my life! But there were many times, Gloria, when I thought this school would never make it. Many times when I was overwhelmed. When I first took over this school, I was so young. Nothing but a mere girl fresh out of Boston College. Barely older than you are now, when the diocese sent me over. All Saints was nothing like it is now. No, it was not nearly such an important institution. In fact, it was little more than a one-room schoolhouse. We had the land, yes, but all around us nothing but bush. The one thing that stood out for me that morning, when I took up this job, was that carrion tree. Said-same one in front of the cafeteria. Gnarled and bent and old as it was. Bright pinkish white tropical flowers, and the stink of that fruit! It's a rare tree in most of the Caribbean, you know, and I thought it auspicious that I should see this tree right here on the land for the new school. I just knew that as long that tree lived, as long as it thrived, All Saints would be alright; the school would thrive. That tree has pushed its roots far down into the soil of the school, and if it could stand strong against all the abuse heaped on it over the years, against hurricanes, floods and torrential down-pours, against droughts, winds and the threat of lightning striking it, if it could stand strong against all of that, then so could I. So *would* I. And you? What's your connection to the tree?"

"I don't quite know. I've just always been glad it is here. Eyesore that people say it is."

"Yes. It's a most seductive little creature, that tree. If you take the time to look at it, to *really* look at it, it's amazing what you will

167

see. In fact, it is quite a lovely tree. The trouble is, Gloria, most people don't take the time to look … Feeling better now?" She looked such a small woman then. A tiny woman in fact. Over the years I had always thought of her as a big, strong, woman. But I saw she was small, frail. I now towered over her.

"Sister, I have something to tell you," I blurted out. An anguished look came over her face, and I could see she was fearing the worst.

"I have decided … I have decided to stay in Jamaica. To go to university here."

Sister Marie Claire laughed. "Gloria, is that it? I thought for a while you were going to tell me something completely different!"

"There is more," I added and she stopped laughing.

"There is someone… someone I have grown quite close to."
"A boy."

"Sister, I want to marry him."

The room went absolutely quiet. "You're not in any trouble are you? Because if you have gone and gotten yourself in trouble …"

"Oh, no, no," I hastened to reassure her. "No, nothing at all like that!"

"Well that's a relief!" She paused, searching for the right words. "You're so young, Gloria. So very young. With a husband usually comes children and then all sorts of responsibilities. Have you given thought to all of that?"

"I have, Sister. I am very sure."

"And Annie, does she know about this?"

Judas. Judas. Judas Iscariot!

"You should tell her, you know," Sister Marie Claire said after a while, "she needs to know."

There were so many things I'd kept secret from Annie. I hadn't even told her about the time I'd gone back to see the recruiter from the college in Minnesota. How I'd asked about housing for married students. How the recruiter had provided me with brochures and her telephone number just in case I had any further questions. How one Sunday, out of sheer boredom, I filled out and sent in an application to the college in Minnesota, but checked "no" to housing for married students. Why I had done that I still did not know – check "no" to housing for married students – but it seemed the right thing to do. No, I hadn't told Annie any of this.

"Poor Annie," Sister Marie Claire was saying. "Poor, poor Annie. She has built her own life around you. Has all her plans centred around the two of you. She will be so disappointed. So very disappointed. *Somebody* should say something to her. Poor, poor Annie."

That evening, curled up on the sofa, watching television, taking a much-needed break from studying and thinking a great deal about what had transpired in Sister Marie Claire's office, there was a knock at the door. Annie was standing outside. She looked very upset and seemed to have been crying for hours. Her eyes were swollen almost shut and her entire face flushed red.

"What is it, Annie?" I asked her, a sinking feeling in the pit of my stomach, because I knew what it would be about. When I had left Sister Marie Claire's office, I'd promised myself I would tell Annie about my plans first thing the following morning.

"Say it's not true! Say it's not true, Gloria! Say none of what Sister Marie Claire told me is true!"

I did not know what to say or do. Mama, hearing the commotion, came to hear what was going on and my heart sank for I had not said anything to her either.

"Gloria, answer me!" Annie was stamping her feet. "When I went in to see Sister Marie Claire... Started talking about us going off together to Canada... L'Université de Laval... Told Sister Marie Claire that my grandparents had even filled out the affidavits for you. That was when she took a deep breath ... that was when she told me! Perhaps I needed to talk to you. Perhaps you had plans of your own! Is it true, Gloria? Is it really true?"

Mama, standing there, looked dumbstruck.

"Annie," I started reaching for her, but she backed away.

"Say it's not true!" she demanded in a terrible pained wail. "Say none of this is true!"

My mother, looking as if she really could not deal with this, backed away from us and left the room.

"Annie, let me explain."

She was weeping really hard now. "Oh Gloria," she said after

169

a while, "Gloria, Gloria, Gloria." She had a frightfully shattered look on her face, and it was then that I understood what lay hiding in Annie's far corners. Hiding deep-deep insider of her. What had always been fragile and vulnerable, curled up there.

"Annie, listen." I was reaching again for her, but she kept backing away, shaking her head in disbelief. Too late I saw that for her everything was falling apart. She looked at me as if she didn't quite know me – had never known me – and turned around and fled. She looked like someone who had suffered a blow from which she would never quite recover.

For hours after that I kept calling and calling Annie's house, trying to talk to her, trying to talk to anyone, but for the first time in all the years I'd been calling that house no one came to the phone. Finally, after many hours, I got a hold of her mother who said that Annie had come home in quite a state. Dishevelled and shaking. Did I know what had happened? What had happened to leave her in such a state? I could not answer.

The next morning I rushed to school, hoping Annie would be there and that I could talk to her, sort things out with her, but Annie was not in school that day. Or the day after. Or the day after. I phoned her mother who told me Annie would not be coming back to school for the rest of the year. She'd had a breakdown, had to be given sedatives; for days she'd been drifting in and out of sleep. Later, her mother told me she kept recounting the same dream: a woman ahead of her on a street. From the shape of the woman she knew the woman was someone she was familiar with, someone she knew very well, but she could never make out the woman's face. She kept walking after the woman, calling her, but no matter how fast she walked, or how much she called, the woman would never turn around and she could never see the woman's face. Exhausted, she sat down under a yellow poui tree and watched as the woman disappeared.

"I don't know what went on between you two, Gloria," Annie's mother said, "but something has really hurt her."

I couldn't begin to explain.

When I was finally allowed to visit Annie, I was shocked at what I saw: a rail thin girl in a white cotton nightgown rocking back and forth, her arms wrapped tight around herself, as if she was trying to keep warm. She was not eating, her mother said, was being prescribed powerful tranquillizers by the doctor, who had even raised the question of taking her into the hospital.

When I visited, her mother and a helper were always at her side. Annie never spoke, but her mother kept asking me what had happened between us? What had gone so terribly wrong? I kept lying and saying I did not know what had happened to Annie.

After several weeks Annie started feeling a little better. One day I found her propped up in a chair by the window, a troubled look on her face, seemingly deep in thought. She would barely look at me.

"How long have I been sick?" she asked.

"About six weeks," her mother said. She looked at me, no doubt wondering why we didn't speak when I visited. How come we had absolutely nothing to say to each other?

"Six weeks!" Annie croaked. "My examinations!"

"You need rest." Her mother was immediately on her feet beside her. "No need to think about those exams."

God, I felt awful. It was so hard to see someone who had been so feisty, so full of life, nothing now but a cut and curled up flower. I started thinking about all the things we had done together, Annie and I, all the fun we'd had. So close, we'd been so close. Despite my best efforts, there were times I would burst into tears in her room, and she would just look over at me, as if I was someone she did not quite know, before looking back out the window.

A few months before this happened, a new guidance teacher had come to work at All Saints. I didn't get to know her very well, for she wasn't at the school long, having gotten herself into trouble with the school's administration, but I'd never met anyone quite like this woman before in my life. She was tall and thin, with straw-coloured hair, and eyes the colour of the afternoon sky. Before coming to All Saints she'd lived all over the place. She wore floral and calico dresses that flapped around her when she walked, big pieces of jade and silver jewellery. She carried herself in a way that let you know that she really didn't care what people thought about her. She'd long figured out who she was, what she wanted to do with her life, and was intent on doing just that. When she came to All Saints she was handed a syllabus to teach from. At first, she made halfhearted attempts at following it, but after a while she put the syllabus aside and brought all sorts of new and interesting materials into the classroom. She was a revelation; it was the first time I'd met someone who seemed so – how can I best describe her? – *regardless* of society. She brought to class an entire packet of what she called *women's poetry*. These poems were a revelation. Here were people talking about things I felt, things I knew, things that went right to the bone. More and more I found myself thinking that I too wanted to do something with words. Would love to be able to do with words what some of these women were doing. Perhaps even then, I knew I wanted to become a writer. Annie resented this teacher who, she felt, was imposing alien and foreign ideas upon us. "Who are all these people?" she complained, looking with distaste at the packet of poems the woman had brought to class, "What about our own writers? Our own teachers?" she asked, thumbing through the poems.

"Don't you see we're in a struggle for our minds," she'd said in exasperation at the no doubt enthusiastic look on my face when I recited one of the poems to her outside of class. "If we don't read our *own* writers *here* in Jamaica, well, where are we *ever* going to read them?"

I'd disagreed with Annie and told her so. My teachers did not have to be like me, did not have to look like me, heck they did not even have to sound like me, for me to learn from them. And then I said something to Annie, that, honestly, I did not know where the words came from; I said: *I am not one of those people who worship at the temple of only one God.*

It was this woman and all her journeys, both within and outside herself, that I began to think very seriously about.

## CHAPTER 15

There is a story of the rivermumma that not many people tell. This is the story, Uncle Silas-Nathaniel says, that we Jamaicans carry inside ourselves.

In olden days, in Stewart Town, high in the mountains of St. Ann, there lived a river-maid named Dora. Dora inhabited a pool that bubbled up from some invisible underground source, and from this pool she formed many rivers. On full moon nights, when the people of Stewart Town were in their homes contemplating their individual worries, Dora would climb on a rock in the centre of the pool, comb her long green hair and sing. The song she sang was sad and haunting, and although the song had no words, to all those who desired the things they'd never had, the meaning of the song was clear: It was an invitation to come to the pool. Their presence would frighten Dora who would leap into the pool, leaving her comb behind, though her song would continue from under the water to the ear of the lucky one who caught the comb. If they returned the comb to her, Dora would grant them their heart's desire. But, it was said, long ago Dora had swum away from Stewart Town, swum away from the source of the river, and made her way out to sea and was never seen by anyone in Stewart Town again. However, since then, people in other parts of the island had reported seeing her combing her long green hair on rocks in various other rivers, in the Martha Brae, the Rio Grande, the Black River, and, in more recent times, on Pim Rock in the Rio Cobre. Wherever she is spotted, she sits on the rocks singing her songs of individual dreams.

I was leaving the island. A couple weeks before, I graduated from All Saints with the highest honours. I won all the major prizes, including the Headmistress's Shield, presented to me by an adoring Sister Marie Claire. Mama, Grandy and Zekie were at the graduation, Mama and Grandy shedding tears of joy, and Zekie looking on proudly. Rafael was there too and I saw Mama looking over at him. Was she softening a little towards him? Both she and Grandy had made it very clear they thought I was making the wrong decision in planning to get married, that I was making a terrific mistake – I was still so young. Grandy was even fiercer than Mama, telling me not to marry Rafael because I really did not know what I was getting myself into; marriage was serious-serious business. I listened to them both without saying a word. This made them even angrier, because they took my silence as resolution, when the truth was I did not really know what I wanted to do.

My graduation should have been one of the happiest days of my life, but my guilt over Annie and what I'd destroyed kept gnawing away at me. Every day, I missed Annie terribly. She was still so sick; had not returned to school. Her parents now talked of taking her to Canada, where, they felt, she would get better care, for she did not seem to be making any progress here on the island.

When the examination results came out later in the summer, no one was surprised I'd passed my exams with distinctions. Scholarship offers poured in from colleges in several countries. For a while I feigned being overwhelmed and said I did not know which one to choose. But all along I knew I would be going to the American college in the place few people on the island had ever heard of: Minnesota. I needed to be in a place where I did not know anyone, and where no one knew me. Minnesota sounded like just such a place. I did not know what I was going to do with my life, I only knew that I no longer wanted to become a medical doctor. Now I wanted to do something with words, with literature. I could not forget those poems that the guidance counsellor had shared with us. Annie did not even blink when I told her about my choice of college. She seemed, in fact, to have been expecting it.

"I bet that boy, Rafael, has something to do with this," she said, turning her head away from me, believing that Rafael was the real cause of what had happened between us. In reality, my choice had nothing to do with Rafael, indeed my college choice had made an irreparable breach in our relationship. Rafael was going to the university here in Jamaica. He had decided long ago that his life was on the island, while right now, I needed a place to figure out all the things that were now turned upside down inside me, and this had to be off the island, away from all that I knew. In my heart, I knew that Grandy and Mama were right. I had a lot more to discover before I settled down with anyone, but I could not admit this to them. As had happened with Annie, my relationship with Rafael began to feel constricting. I needed space. So much space now. And distance. Rafael and I made some halfhearted promises to keep in touch, to write to each other, but the last time at the botanical gardens when we kissed and touched and when I finally allowed him all the way inside my body (my-friends-and-I-always-have-*something*-on-us), we both knew this was the last time we would be seeing each other.

"So you are really going away?" he asked.

"Yes," I told him.

"And there is really nothing I can do?"

"I'm afraid not."

He looked at me long and hard then. "You've changed," he said. "You're not the same girl I met a year and a half ago."

I laughed a wry little laugh. "By that do you mean I have a mind now? My *own* mind? That I can think and think things through by myself?"

He did not answer.

"Ah, Rafael," I said, and felt myself very close to tears, "everyone and everything needs to grow, to change from time to time."

He turned then and looked at me and I could see that he was sad, hurt and disappointed too. Then he said something that took the scales off my eyes, let me see perhaps much too clearly that it just would not have ever worked out between us.

"Gloria, I want a woman who will never change. Who will be the same year after year. I don't want someone who says they are going to do one thing and ends up doing just another. Like someone who went away and never came back to Jamaica. Someone who left a woman waiting year after year for him here in Jamaica, while he went and made his life with another. I want someone – a woman – who will be the same person ten, fifteen, twenty years from now."

My eyes clouded over and I started to sob. "Well then, Rafael, I guess I am not the right woman for you."

We said nothing to each other after that.

As for my mother, she and I pretty much kept to ourselves in the house. Barely touching, barely speaking to each other. In the same way that Annie felt I had betrayed her, Mama evidently felt the same. All the while I was packing, throwing things out and buying new things to take with me to America, Mama never once asked me about my plans. Now, so many years later, looking back at it, I can finally understand her attitude. If I had not felt the need to tell her what I was doing all along, why should she bother to ask me now?

A few days before I left, I went to spend some time with Grandy. On the surface, nothing much had changed, yet everything was changing. Junie was still living with her parents, but talked ever more of leaving, of going somewhere else, maybe to get work in Kingston. Sophie was preparing for her final examinations, and Monique was working in a store in the Bay. I told them about seeing Yvette, how she had written to me telling me Grenada was not quite what she'd expected and she was thinking about moving on, maybe either Trinidad or Barbados, she wasn't sure which one yet. I knew she would never stop moving, until she made her way to New York, where she would search and search for her mother.

Smiles came over my friends' faces when I told them about Yvette, and I guessed they were thinking about the times we had spent together as children. Now it seemed such an innocent, idyllic time, our days in the river.

On my last night in the country, Grandy came to me and said, "Gloria, here is something I want you to have. Something I have been working on for you, for a long time. Something to keep you warm when the nights get too cold."

It was a shawl. A lilac shawl.

She must have known about all the things that were going on inside me, things that I could not put into words. For even to myself, to say nothing of those around me, I had grown sullen and defensive. At nights I could barely sleep and in the mornings I would wake up tired and feverish, as if I had spent the entire night fighting.

Grandy must have sensed all this, because she just let me be. She left me alone to wander from place to place, touching plants, smelling flowers, going to sit silently in Uncle Silas' field as he worked. Neither of us said anything much to the other. I went to the river, laid on my back and watched the water flow. I could have done this forever. I envied the river's certainty, the sense that it knew where it was going on its tried and true path to the sea.

"I also want you to know," Grandy said, reaching down to squeeze the tip of my nose as she'd done so many times when I was a child, "that I'm going to miss you terribly when you leave, but I am so proud of you, so very, very proud of you."

Back in Kingston I went to the yard to say my goodbyes. I did not know half of the people now living there. Miss Sarah had been moved to an old people's home. Miss Christie was grudgingly watching her now-three grandchildren, while Denise went to work. And Nadia was still there, still struggling with Jesus and her children. New people were in the house where I used to live, and where Miss Sarah and Rachel had lived, what seemed to me now a long, long time ago. People had slipped into the places and spaces we used to occupy. Yes, so much had changed and so much had not changed.

On the day I left, I did not want anyone to come with me to the airport. This was something I wanted to do alone. I looked around one last time at my room. Everything was neatly in its place, and all the drawers and closets were empty. Anyone, seeing how thoroughly I had cleaned out the room, could have been forgiven for thinking I had no intention of ever coming back. I carried my suitcases downstairs, left them at the front door and came back up to my mother's room. She was inside, pretending to be busy dusting and tidying up an already spotless room. She barely looked up at me when I came in.

"I'm about to go," I said to her.

"I know," she answered in a sad, sombre voice. She turned around to face me and we stood there looking at each other. Finally she spoke, and she seemed to be having great difficulty with the words. "You are my daughter." She held out her hands to me.

"And you are my mother," I replied, moving into her arms.

"Yes, I am your mother."

She looked down at her hands, turning them this way then that, examining them in detail as if to see if they gave any clue about what had happened to us. She had raised me with those hands and, I could see it clearly then for the first time in my life, she had done her very best by me. She sighed heavily, a sigh that said there were many things being left unsaid. She could not understand why I was doing this, why I felt the need to go so far away. And if she had asked me, she would have discovered that I did not really know the answer. All I knew was that I needed to leave, to go to a place far, far away.

"Well," I said, looking down at my watch, hoping to stop the tears gathering in my eyes, "it's time for me to go. Give Zekie my regards." He had mysteriously disappeared at the time of my goodbyes. Over the years I had come to accept him, had even come to develop a fierce kind of fondness for him. Now I would say, to anyone who asked, that Zekie and I were friends, *despite* how he had made his money. He had made it very clear to me a couple of days before that if I needed anything, anything at all, I was not to hesitate to ask him, for he would do for me whatever he could do for me. He had bought me my plane ticket and given me the American money I now had in my pocket.

"Yes," Mama answered, smiling bravely through her tears, "it's time for you to go. Please give Annie my regards." She knew I would be making a stop at Annie's house, before heading for the airport.

"I will," I said, and looked at her for a very long time. I wanted to fill my mind with her. I wanted to tell her that I loved her, that I was thankful for all the things she had done for me, all the sacrifices I knew she had made on my behalf, but I was having the greatest difficulty getting any words out.

"I know, Gloria," she said after a while, her head dropping and looking away from me. "I know."

At that moment, if my mother had asked me to stay, just told me to stay, I would have. If the words had come out of her mouth at that moment that I should stay, God knows I would not have gone. I was looking for some reason, any reason at all, not to go away. But she did not say any such thing.

Mama brought her hand up to her mouth and stifled a cry. She gave me another fierce protective hug. "Here," she said, "I have something for you." It was a gold chain with a pendant of a bird with an aquamarine beak, and small red rubies for eyes. It perfectly matched the earrings she had given me so many years before when I first passed my common entrance examination; earrings I was now wearing.

"I have kept this chain for you for years," she said, fixing the chain about my neck. "I used to say to myself: I will give this chain to my daughter when she is going off to college, when she is going out into the world. So there, now, I've given you the chain, you, my daughter. Now you go on!" she said, pushing me through the door, pushing me away from her, sending me out into the world. "You have a plane to catch. I only want you to remember two things, my daughter: you always have a home; and you always have a mother."

I hurried out of the room after that, because I knew that soon she would collapse in tears, and I did not want to see her crying even more.

Outside, the taxi driver helped me put my suitcases in the trunk of the car. All the way over to Annie's house, I kept dreading what I would say to her. She still barely spoke to me, and there was an ever-present sadness in her hazel-green eyes. Annie's mother let me in and took me up to her room, where she was again "resting". Though she didn't say anything, the look Annie's mother's gave me could not help being an accusing one. She had known from the start that whatever had happened to Annie, involved me. But neither of us was saying anything and she was still none the wiser.

Annie was standing near the window, her back to me, and she turned ever so slightly when I came into the room. She turned just enough so I could see the profile of her face. Her mother withdrew and left us alone.

"I am leaving."

"I know," she said, in a small sad voice.

We stood there, neither of us saying anything. Finally she spoke, and a sob passed her lips. "Now you take care of yourself."

Oh, how I wanted to run to her, to put my arms around her, to hold her tight. I wanted us to be the two girls who had pledged to never forsake each other. I wanted our lives to go back to what they had been so many years before. But we were both women now, and had individual choices to make.

Neither of us made the move to come any closer to the other. This had been the girl I had grown up with, the girl I had done just about everything with. I loved her dearly and I could not believe we were saying goodbye to each other.

"Well," I said finally, "it's time for me to go." The feelings that had been dogging me, threatening to overwhelm me, the amorphous gray fog hovering about my head, was pressing in close on me again. I had to get out of the room. I had to get off this island. I had to get away.

"Yes," she answered softly, looking out the window, "your car is waiting and you have to go." She seemed to be assessing something about her life, something that did not make any sense to her. The room went gray, storm clouds were gathering.

"Gloria," she called out when I was at the door.

"Yes?" I turned around to look at her.

She made as if to say something to me, but thought the better of it. "Just you remember to take good care of yourself."

I walked away, promising myself not to turn and look back at her, because I knew if I did, I would, like Lot's wife, dissolve into a pillar of salt. Outside it started drizzling, and before long it was raining – softly at first, before coming down harder and harder, threatening to obscure the majestic blue mountains.

Oh those dark blue mountains, I always did and always would love those dark blue mountains; and the girl at the window, I would always love, always remember her too. Despite myself, I did look back. Annie was still at the window looking out, almost hidden in the darkness, repeatedly bringing her hands to her face.

Inside the taxi I reached into my travelling bag and pulled out the lilac shawl my grandmother had given to me, and threw it over my shoulders. On my lap I placed the emerald green box I'd taken from Rachel's room. Inside the box were my passport, my plane ticket, and a faded black and white photograph of my mother.

# ABOUT THE AUTHOR

Jacqueline Bishop was born in Kingston, Jamaica. Her parents separated early in her life, and she lived for many years with her mother and (then three) siblings, but lived with her father for several years when her mother migrated to the United States. She grew up in Kingston, but as a child spent her summer holidays in the district of Nonsuch, deep in the mountains of Portland. There she moved easily among the homes of her (maternal) great grandparents, her grandparents and numerous aunts, uncles and cousins. Nonsuch, at that time, was a place of 'no electricity' and she passed many evenings on the verandah of her great grandparents' home, listening to the stories and folk legends of Jamaica.

After completing Holy Childhood High School, she joined her mother in the USA to attend Lehman College, City University of New York, and later completed a Master's in poetry writing at New York University. in 1998.

In 1997 she received a scholarship to the Oral History Summer Program at Columbia University and her work on the oral histories of Jamaican women living in New York City was published by Africa World Press in June 2006 as, *My Mother Who Is Me: Lifestories from Jamaican Women in New York*.

She pursued a (second) Master's of Fine Arts degree in fiction writing at NYU, and while still a graduate student founded, and is presently the editor for *Calabash: A Journal of Caribbean Arts and Letters*, which publishes creative and critical writing on and from the Anglophone, Francophone, Hispanic and Dutch-speaking Caribbean. She started production on a film, *I Came Here By A Dream: The Jamaican Intuitive Artists*. For this work, she received several fellowships at NYU, culminating in the Arthur Schomburg Award for Excellence in the Humanities in 2000.

Ms. Bishop has published in *Callalloo: A Journal of African-American and African Arts and Letters*, *Crab Orchard Review*, *Wasafiri*, *Die Aussensites Des Elementes*, *Fairchild Publications*, *The Caribbean Writer*, *Unfold Magazine*, *MACO: Caribbean Living*, *Calabash: A Journal of Caribbean Arts and Letters*. She taught literature at Medgar Evers College, was Writer-in-Residence at Teachers and Writers Collaborative, and has served as a facilitator for Women in Literature and Letters, a collective devoted to social change and action by women through the written word. Presently, she teaches writing at New York University. She lives in New York City.

## ALSO BY JAQUELINE BISHOP

*Fauna*
ISBN: 1-84523-032-9; pp: 84; pub. July 2006; price: £7.99

Using metaphors drawn from the fauna and flora of Jamaica and images drawn from the visual arts, Bishop explores the tensions between plenitude and emptiness, presence and absence, the nourishing and the poisonous in her memories of the rural Jamaican childhood that has shaped her.

From the perspective of New York, Bishop sees herself as another kind of fauna, the Jamaican birds which can be found everywhere, 'identified from the peculiar way they sing.' This is a moving and heart-felt collection, but Bishop never allows the siren voice of longing for return to become sentimental. Always there is the drive towards the artist's desire to remake the world and to work meticulously at what can be left in, what must be taken out.

"To render the familiar strange and new again is the task of gifted poets. Jacqueline Bishop's poems do this in wonderful ways. She calls upon powerful sources, including world mythology, her own Jamaican ancestry and her full-woman experiences to create these fabulous, shining songs of innocence, loss, birth, rebirth, wit and wisdom. Good job Miss Jacqueline!"

— LORNA GOODISON, author of *Controlling the Silver*

"Jacqueline Bishop's debut collection offers us passage into other worlds, both geographical and mythical. These poems define family, home, longing, and exile in profoundly moving and refreshingly new ways. They capture a myriad of voices, from those of the elders to those of the "Fauna" that populate the gorgeous second section of the book. The voices and images Bishop constructs in these poems are haunting in the best possible way: they are the melody we hear that reminds us of who we are, where we are from, and where we are going."

— SHARA McCALLUM, author of *Song of Thieves*.

JUST OUT...

Opal Palmer Adisa
*Until Judgement Comes: Stories about Jamaican Men*
ISBN: 184523 042 6; pp. 258; pub. Feb. 2007; £8.99

The stories in this collection move the heart and the head. They concern the mystery that is men: men of beauty who are as cane stalks swaying in the breeze, men who are afraid of and despise women, men who prey on women, men who have lost themselves, men trapped in sexual and religious guilt, men who love women and men who are searching for their humanity...

The stories are framed by the memories of an old Jamaican woman about the community that has grown up around her. The seven stories are structured around wise sayings that the community elder remembers as her grandfather's principle legacy, concerning the nature of judgement, both divine and human. Each story uses a saying as the starting point but the stories are far from illustrative tracts. From Devon aka Bad-Boy growing up with an abusive mother, to Ebenezer, a single man mysteriously giving birth to a child, to the womanizer Padee whose many women and children struggle to resolve issues with their father, each story reveals the complex, and often painful, introspective search of these men.

All Peepal Tree titles are available from the website
**www.peepaltreepress.com**
with a money back guarantee, secure credit card ordering
and fast delivery throughout the world at cost or less.

Peepal Tree Press is celebrated as the home of challenging and inspiring literature from the Caribbean and Black Britain. Visit www.peepaltreepress.com to read sample poems and reviews, discover new authors, established names and access a wealth of information. Subscribe to our mailing list for news of new books and events.

Contact us at:
Peepal Tree Press, 17 King's Avenue, Leeds LS6 1QS, UK
Tel: +44 (0) 113 2451703 E-mail: contact@peepaltreepress.com